MURDER IN BARBADOS

MURDER IN BARBADOS

A Jamie Prescott Mystery

Mariann Tadmor

Copyright © 2004 by Mariann Tadmor.

ISBN: Hardcover   1-4134-5576-X
          Softcover   1-4134-5575-1

All rights reserved. No part of this book may be reproduced or transmitted in any form or by any means, electronic or mechanical, including photocopying, recording, or by any information storage and retrieval system, without permission in writing from the copyright owner.

This is a work of fiction. Names, characters, places and incidents either are the product of the author's imagination or are used fictitiously, and any resemblance to any actual persons, living or dead, events, or locales is entirely coincidental.

This book was printed in the United States of America.

To order additional copies of this book, contact:
Xlibris Corporation
1-888-795-4274
www.Xlibris.com
Orders@Xlibris.com

24009

For my family, near and far,
with love

ACKNOWLEDGEMENTS

I am greatly indebted to my editor, Yoav Tadmor, whose dedication and support made this a better book.

CHAPTER 1

'The first body washed up on the beach at daybreak. The second came in half an hour later a kilometer further to the north. Two constables at the scene reported that the bodies of the men had been in the water only long enough to be gouged by coral and have their long hair tangled in seaweed. No positive identification has been made.'

You either have it or you don't. And I have it. A talent for landing in trouble, that is.

But when I sat in the air and looked down at the coastline of Barbados I had almost forgotten about the newspaper article. Up above, white castles, drifting on a carpet of azure blue, floated majestically past my eyes—castles with turrets and gables, towers and ramparts, stacked in tiers of cloudy formations.

Below, the sea was a clear blue topaz with coral reefs showing through a shiny path of sunlight. Reflections of clouds lay on the ocean surface in immovable dark blotches and, close to the coast, sailboats and wind surfers floated and dipped like large moths fluttering their wings in the wind. A string of green atolls lined the bay where a valley cut into the land near the airport.

Last night Bob Makowski, my fellow private investigator and former boss, had brought me the *Barbados Advocate*. After seeing the headline I had pushed the paper across my desk to him.

"Where did you get this?" I said.

"Picked it up downtown especially for you."

"Doesn't seem like the most peaceful vacation spot," I said.

Bob had grabbed the paper, glanced briefly at the headline *Macabre Find Near Holetown*, and turned to the middle pages.

"Here," he said and stabbed a finger at a respectable size ad. "That's what you're supposed to be looking at."

The Colonial Travel Agency, Bridgetown, it said. *Proprietor Louise Higginbotham. Scuba-diving, biking and hiking tours. Individuals and groups. Personal attention.*

"Isn't that what you have in mind? Scuba-diving and biking?" Bob said.

"It is. Still," I had persisted because—as Bob kindly points out to whoever will listen—I won't let go of a good argument. "Still, two bodies washing up on the beach right near my luxury hotel makes me wonder."

"Jamie Prescott." Bob had sounded exasperated. "I know what you'll say next. That it's my fault for suggesting Barbados to you."

It was true, though. After my recent caper at Machu Picchu Bob had suggested I make some routine inquiries in Barbados on behalf of one of his clients and I had agreed. When it turned out the inquiry was no longer necessary I had decided to go anyway. I needed an entirely private, relaxing vacation.

"No, it's not your fault. I should really thank you."

"I'm waiting."

"Oh, okay, thank you."

I had looked again at the ad in the *Barbados Advocate*. "I guess it can't hurt to e-mail this Louise Higginbotham to sign up for scuba-diving and line up a mountain bike." And that's what I'd done.

The plane now made a wide turn, I glimpsed a long stretch of sand, my heart skipped a beat and the tiny hairs on my arms bristled. A shiver of excitement ran through me. A real vacation at last.

The Grantley Adams International Airport teemed with tourists, all in shorts, straw hats and, in the case of those departing, glorious sun tans. Cheerful porters pushed luggage-carts around and a constant low-voiced chatter hummed through the hall.

I had booked a beach cottage at a hotel near Holetown. The plush chauffeured car sent by the hotel took me north from the airport through the small towns of Oistins, Dover, Worthing, and Hastings, the names transporting me to England and conjuring up images of the small group of British settlers which came to Barbados in 1627. Twenty years later, so the books had told me, their sugar plantations had converted the island into the wealthiest colony in the new world.

The narrow road filled up with buses, minibuses, cabs and private cars, to the point where we slowed down to well under the hourly speed limit which was set at a heady thirty miles. The buses stopped leisurely at very short intervals and we were all stuck behind them. I looked out the window and into the brown, moist eyes of a cow grazing tranquilly on a small patch of grass right on the side of the highway.

"Tek time en' laziness," my driver singsang, which I took as a sign that I should slow down, too, mentally and physically. I took several deep breaths and forced myself to relax.

The hotel proved as good as its reputation, utterly luxurious. The car carried me smoothly up the circular driveway to a low-slung building whose coral stone facade glimmered in the blinding sunlight. The air was perfumed by scarlet poinsettias, yellow jasmine, and white orchids.

My cottage, one of several set in a luscious garden amidst coconut palms and banana plants, sat separate from the main hotel building and faced the beach. It had a spacious living room, a large bedroom with a view, a bathroom with a Jacuzzi, and a kitchenette with a microwave. The best part was no doubt the porch, furnished with lounge chairs from where I imagined I'd have a spectacular view of the rising sun.

There was a knock at the door and the maid assigned to make my stay comfortable, entered with a cheerful "Good evening."

"Good evening," I said, even though it was only three in the afternoon.

She was all white teeth and fat cheeks and said her name was Penelope. She fluffed my pillows, left extra towels, and generally buzzed about the cottage being helpful. When she left I changed into my new black bikini and wrap purchased at Saks Fifth Avenue in Chevy Chase under the watchful eye of Topsy—my partner at the Bethesda travel agency we bought when I retired as Bob's full-time investigator and became his occasional snoop. Topsy is also my former college room mate, mother of two, married to Jack Bannister, an attorney in Washington, D.C.

"Have you heard from Archibald Brewster?" had been her parting words to me. She had introduced me to this gorgeous man several months ago and we'd had two dinners and one night together before he transferred to his law firm's San Francisco office.

"He left a message on my machine," I said.

"And are you going to see him?"

"Not that I know of."

"But he's so attractive." Topsy had looked as if she'd just tasted something yummy.

"He's attractive in San Francisco and aren't you the one who preaches against long-distance relationships? Or doesn't it apply to Archibald Brewster?"

"There are exceptions. And this is one. I know you like him."

"Okay," I had said in order to get Topsy out of my hair. "If Brewster moves back here permanently I'll reconsider. Does that make you happy?"

"Uhm, er, I suppose."

But right now I was a woman ready for a vacation. My copy of the *Barbados Advocate* still sat on top of my suitcase and I deliberately pushed the thought of the headline out of my mind. Instead I stepped down from the porch and walked towards the beach.

I felt my spirits lift.

CHAPTER 2

The beach stretched from the wooded terrain behind the hotel towards the white foam whipping at the edge of the water. Palm trees stood bent in unlikely positions and provided plenty of shade. Several small palm-thatched roofs on wooden stilts served as way stations for waiters to serve the guests. I put down my towel and sunglasses on a beach chair with a colorful, springy cushion, and set off for a swim equipped with my snorkeling gear.

The hot sand melted away under my bare feet, and the ripples made by the gently lapping sea petered out as I entered the warm, blue-green water. I swam towards a couple of fishing boats pulling at their anchors before I adjusted my goggles, dipped my face, and opened my eyes. The water was clear as crystal and patches of coral jumped up at me, pink, turquoise and blue. Tiny creatures darted about chasing one another, and a school of black and orange-striped fish moved by with languid flutters of translucent tail fins.

I turned around on my back to float with eyes closed against the sun. Tiny spots behind my eyelids moved in step with my heartbeat and all I could hear were the waves clucking rhythmically against the side of one of the fishing boats. The water enveloped me with its warmth and I floated several more minutes while my muscles lost their tension and my mind drifted towards sleep.

I came to when a heavy splash rocked my body and I was submerged by a violent swirl of water. The sea was no longer azure blue and friendly but dark green and menacing. Something sharp seared the entire length of my leg. I wanted to cry out *Shark*. Instead, I took in a mouthful of seawater and choked on it. I twisted and turned, without a weapon but ready to fight, unable to see the enemy, just knowing something was on the attack.

A body rose in the water next to me. I treaded water, unable to reach the bottom of the sea with my feet, gurgling and spluttering, my fingers entangled in something stringy. I pulled and brought up a human face with closed eyes. The body shifted away from me, a sudden wave pushed it back down and I lost my grip. I dove under, my feet found the bottom, and I came back up clutching the unwieldy form.

The body weighed a ton. I turned on my back, held the head between my hands and pushed off with both legs, moving him rescue-fashion, towards shore. It was heavy going. I hadn't realized how far out I was. The waves were breaking more forcefully now, whipping up foam, and I pulled the body closer in an effort to keep the head well above water.

People were gathered on the beach when I got in. The body was pulled away from me while I sat in shallow water gasping for air and coughing up salt. When I got up, a crowd stood around the man on the ground. He was on his stomach, someone was pummeling him between the shoulder blades. There was a retching sound. Seawater streamed from under the face. The arms flailed. The legs pulled him into a fetal position.

I bent over the curled-up body and observed the tangled hair, the wiry body, and a tattoo—of a convulsed cobra—encircling his upper left arm, its forked tongue raised. His eyes were open, he stared straight at me without blinking and without moving. The pupils were mere pin-pricks, the whites streaked with red. Then his lips parted, more water poured out, his upper lip receded and revealed livid red gums and huge teeth. Ugly.

Two equally ugly guys hefted him up by the arms, shook him rather hard, stood him on his feet, and moved him off without as much as a nod at me. The crowd melted away just as fast and I was suddenly alone, surrounded by no one.

I turned to four guys with stringy hair sitting on the sand watching the departing figures, and asked them who I'd rescued but they acted as if I spoke a foreign language. Two skinny women behind huge sunglasses shook their heads in denial when I asked them if they knew the guy with the tattoo. I gave up. It didn't really matter. I wasn't looking for a medal. But it would have been nice to keep my snorkel, now lost at sea.

I went back to the water and looked at the distance I had swum with the body from somewhere near the two fishing boats. The water shimmered where the sun's rays hit the surface. I shaded my eyes thinking I saw a movement. Was someone in the boat farthest from shore? The shadow disappeared and the boat bobbed up and down on the waves. There was no one there. It must have been the haze.

I shook my head to get water out of my ears. I had suddenly lost my zest for the sea and decided to walk back. My heart was still beating hard and I took a series of deep breaths before starting out.

When I arrived at my own stretch of sand in front of the hotel a few more people were sitting in lounge chairs, their bodies glistening with oil, their faces tilted to the sun. I looked at them feeling alienated, wanting to tell someone of my weird experience, that I had just rescued a fellow being from drowning. But the only person remotely interested in me was the waiter from the hotel who appeared at my side with a tray of snacks.

"Good evening, de day pretty, pretty, pretty. The seabath good, good, good?"

I stared at him and wanted to say, no, it was all bad, bad, bad.

"Why, yes, very good, thank you," I said, instead, and smiled at his round dark face.

"You need ma'be guide tomorrow? Or ma'be some white stuff?"

"*What?*"

He looked down at me with cool eyes. Evaluating.

"What did you say?" I shook my head.

"You drinkin' rum or ma'be fruit juice?" He had evaluated and found me wanting.

"I'll have a rum punch. And make that double rum," I said and he promised to bring me one fast, fast, fast. Which he did.

I gulped it down and the rum hit my stomach like a rolling stone.

"This is all your fault, Bob Makowski," I muttered under my breath.

I sat there with my eyes closed re-playing the reel. The body in the water, my hands entangled in stringy hair, the white face, the ugly teeth. Looked European. A drifter? The headline in the *Barbados Advocate* leapt to my mind and I had a hazy notion that I should inform the police but didn't know quite of what. I heard Topsy's voice saying 'must you always get yourself in trouble?' and then my mother declaring that the best place for my vacation would be a desert island.

When I woke up the beach was almost empty. I heard the bell-like sounds of a Bajan steel band somewhere in the distance. I stood up, shaded my eyes against the setting sun and looked down the beach towards the two fishing boats. They were gone.

At the cottage a message was blinking on the answering machine. Louise Higginbotham wanted to speak to me.

CHAPTER 3

Louise Higginbotham's persona was an eye-opener. I'm not sure what I'd expected but there she was at the front desk of the *Colonial Travel Agency*. She looked at me from piercing blue eyes on either side of an impressive Romanesque nose jutting from her high forehead. She wet her protruding teeth—moist in the first place—and I'll be forgiven if my first thought was 'horse.' She got up from her desk, whinnied, and trotted towards me.

"I'm Jamie Prescott," I said. "I got your message last night so I presume you received my e-mail about scuba-diving and biking?"

"Yes, indeed, I did, and that's what I wanted to talk to you about. We could have done this by phone, of course."

"That's all right. I wanted to take a look at Bridgetown, anyway."

"And now I can give you these in person."

She handed me a brochure and a confirmation slip which indicated that I was signed up with a watersports operator for a week of daily two-tank dives. All I had to do was show up and ask for someone called Beth.

"Super," I said.

After watching the sun rise in the morning—and enjoying a Continental breakfast on the porch—I had picked up my rental car which the attentive hotel people had delivered to the parking lot. I had arrived in Bridgetown after a harrowing half hour on the left-hand side of the road and decided to park at the first available spot.

After I traversed National Heroes Square—formerly Trafalgar Square—with the statue of Nelson perched on top of a small wedding cake, a policeman in bell-bottom trousers and a white tropical helmet had encouraged me to cross the road. He pirouetted languidly and halted traffic on my behalf. Very colonial. Slow motion permeated the very air.

The buildings had red awnings and shuttered windows. Fishing boats, sailboats, and yachts dotted the harbor, and street vendors sat under shadowy trees selling bananas, coconuts, and woven baskets. Cars moved along sedately on the wrong side of the street.

Two small flags, one British and one Barbadian—the latter a black trident on a yellow and royal blue background—fluttered in the brisk air outside the travel agency. The windows on either side of the door were dark and I wondered how prospective travelers found the incentive to enter. I would have arranged for a few well-placed spotlights and some enticing travel posters.

The interior of the agency was not much brighter. Strange for an island bathed in almost perpetual sun. The three desks were of massive mahogany, and dark bookcases stacked with brochures lined the walls. A couple of posters showed English landscapes, castles, and lush green cricket fields. This was obviously a business geared mostly towards travel away from Barbados.

"I saw your ad in the *Barbados Advocate* just the day before I left Washington and thought I'd advance my reservations by a couple of days," I now said and sat down in the chair Louise Higginbotham offered me.

"Yes, and I'm most awfully glad you did." Her voice was crisp and British. "Everyone is quite booked up that's why I couldn't fit you in until Wednesday."

"That's fine."

"And I am arranging for a mountain bike to be delivered to your hotel. You can keep it for the duration. I understand you'd rather bike off by yourself than join a tour group? I'll leave off some trail maps for you as well."

Louise Higginbotham looked as if she was facing a major decision. Her teeth glinted.

"Would you by any chance like to take a walk with me right now?" she said. "They do say that what I don't know about Barbados isn't worth knowing. You might consider it a professional courtesy from one agent to another."

"Love to," I said without hesitation.

"And do call me Louise." She inserted herself into a mud-colored woollen cardigan. In her sturdy walking shoes she looked as if she was about to set off into foggy London.

"Did you know," she said as soon as we were out in the sun-drenched street. "Did you know that the Amerindians came over from Venezuela and Guyana in about 300 A.D. in their canoes and stayed here until the Spanish slave traders arrived in the 1500s. Then they just melted away, maybe they went back to where they originated. I've always thought that was terribly clever of them."

Louise looked at me with a rather alarming smile. She had a trick of lifting her eyebrows and peering sideways while darting her moist teeth forward.

"And did you know that Bridgetown got its name from a wooden bridge built across Carlisle Bay by those same Amerindians? The British who first came here called it the Indian River Bridge. They constructed vast warehouses and traded sugar, rum, and slaves. But most of the original buildings went up in flames a hundred and fifty years ago."

No doubt about it, whenever Louise started a sentence with 'did you know,' she was about to impart a new nugget of information. And I didn't have to wait long for the next one.

Louise pointed towards the water.

"You know, this is where ships were brought in to have the barnacles scraped off their hulls. It's called the Careenage. And in a moment we will get to St. Michael's Cathedral. You must cross the churchyard to see the frangipani trees in bloom. Elizabeth and I—she's my best friend—often sit on a bench in there, it's so peaceful. But she's in England at the moment."

Louise suddenly looked pre-occupied and we walked on in silence.

"And do you also visit England once in a while?" I asked. I couldn't quite figure out what sort of a person she really was. But with my unfortunate penchant for flights of fancy— a trait Bob Makowski often points out has had detrimental effects on several investigations—I pegged Louise Higginbotham as a repressed virgin dedicated to her job and to her old, gruff military-type father.

"Not any more," Louise said. "But you mustn't think that I have led a very sheltered life here. Before I married and had children—and I have four—I traveled about in Europe by myself. And visited with my father's family in England, some rather remote cousins."

"When did your father come out here?" I said and reluctantly dismissed the virgin and military-type images. "Oh, my father was born here. It was my grandfather who came out from England in 1920, he was with the government. Elizabeth's family, of course, were rich planters from way back and Elizabeth was an only child and inherited the Granger-Farley sugar plantation. It's inland from your hotel. I'll take you there this afternoon if you're interested."

"That would be great. I'd love to see a working plantation."

"*My* parents owned a restaurant in Bridgetown. Lovely parents they were and I was terribly lucky to have the same kind of marriage to my dear Geoffrey. He passed on five years ago."

"I'm so sorry to hear that," I said. "Was that when you started your travel agency?"

"Oh, no, my dear, I've had it for years and years. I began as a secretary to old Mr. Wright—he was a former army colonel—*he* started the agency in 1975. When he retired, I bought him out."

See, an army colonel, I thought, probably old and crusty.

"Tell me more about the sugar plantation," I said. "It conjures up all kinds of romantic notions."

Louise was silent for so long that, for a moment, I thought she hadn't heard me. And when she did answer she wasn't talking about the plantation.

"Elizabeth Granger-Farley is one of my oldest friends. We went to school together. We are like sisters. Of course, her last name isn't Granger-Farley anymore. She became Elizabeth Mattson when she married Hugh, and that was some twenty years ago."

"And when is she returning from England?"

"That's just it." Louise suddenly pulled out a large handkerchief and blew her nose. "I don't know. I had a card from her several months ago saying she would see me soon. Then Hugh returned and said she had stayed behind with relatives. I wrote to the address Hugh gave me but I never heard back and that's not like Elizabeth. And she never stays with relatives, she likes quaint little hotels."

I made some inadequate noises of commiseration and we continued our walk until Louise stopped in front of a large display window in a two-story building. The white sign with gold and red lettering that swayed in the light breeze above the door said *Sunshine Art Gallery*.

"Come inside, if you like, and I'll introduce you to some dear friends of mine," Louise said.

CHAPTER 4

"Jamie Prescott. Meet Noelle Lalue, one of the owners of the gallery," Louise said brightly. And to Noelle she added: "Jamie is a fellow travel agent from the States."

Noelle was in the middle of the room. Tall with wide hips and size eleven feet squeezed into size nine shoes. Glossy hair, straightened and on the verge of crimping up. The handshake she offered me was so firm that I suppressed an involuntary moan. Here was something *tae kwon do* had not prepared me for.

She laughed.

"*Excusé moi!* I didn't mean to hurt you. We're having a special exhibition. Are you interested in Haitian art?"

"You bet I am," I exclaimed. "I was in Haiti a few years ago and have a small collection of paintings at home but I had no idea I would find them in Barbados."

I looked around at the vibrant paintings displayed on the white-washed walls of the gallery. I knew in an instant the one I would buy. It was about sixteen by twenty-four inches, not yet framed, and I immediately recognized the cobalt blue color, the tiny houses, people, and palm trees, a land connected by roads to a globe hovering above symbolizing the earth and the moon. A typical voodoo inspired configuration.

While Noelle attended to a customer, Louise filled me in. It seemed that Noelle had arrived from Martinique about three years ago. And, my dear, said Louise, her English is quite good. Noelle had hooked up with a retired New Yorker by the name of Mel Kramer who had just opened the art gallery.

"And they live together," Louise concluded and glanced at me briefly before turning to Noelle.

"I've been telling Jamie all about you, my dear," she said. "How successful you are. And where is Mel?"

"Right here," boomed a voice from behind and I spun around. Mel Kramer looked the way he sounded. Loud. Tall, lean and brash, with sandy-colored thinning hair, a good tan and teeth to match, and violet blue eyes under hooded lids. He scanned my body quickly and I wondered briefly how involved he was with Noelle. Men's body-scanning usually ticks me off but it was either my recently acquired Caribbean mood or else a certain chemistry between us that made me overlook this one. Mel's handshake left Noelle's in the dust but I was prepared and gave as good as I got. What was it with these expatriates? It was starting to be painful.

I pointed to the painting I'd decided to buy and managed not to flinch when I heard the price.

"An early Prèfête Duffaut," Noelle said. "A very unusual find. Museum quality."

I know an opportunity when I see it and didn't hesitate. "I'll take it."

"I'll deliver it to your hotel," Mel Kramer said.

"Louise, why don't you bring Jamie over for dinner tonight," Noelle said. "I'll have the painting ready for you then."

"I'll pick you up," Mel said and received a withering look from Noelle.

"I'll drive myself," I said. "Might as well practice being left-handed. I'll pick up Louise on the way."

The daggers disappeared from Noelle's eyes, I paid for the painting with my credit card and pocketed the receipt together with the directions to their house. It was not too far from the gallery.

Mel trained his violet eyes on me, pulled out chairs and offered soft drinks from a small refrigerator at the back.

"Or, maybe you'd rather have a rum punch? Mount Gay, the best."

"A bit too early in the day for me," I said.

"Did you know," said Louise, "that it takes about ten tons of sugar cane to make half a bottle of rum?"

I laughed. "No, I did not know that."

Louise moistened her teeth unnecessarily.

"Rum was a favorite of pirates and sailors and I'm afraid they would get terribly drunk. It comes in all shades from white to gold. But you probably know that already. Of course, I don't partake myself. I'll have water. Did you know that we have the world's cleanest drinking water?"

I laughed again, a nervous reaction which by now seemed my only defense against the barrage of information forthcoming from Louise.

"The water comes from the underground lakes within the coral core of the island and is absolutely pure. You must drink as much as you can while you're here."

"I will," I promised and accepted a glass of crystal clear water from Mel. I drank, and it certainly beat the taste of some of the deadened, purified and re-cycled stuff which has begun to pass for spring water at home.

"You should export it," I said.

"Have you heard from Elizabeth yet?" Mel looked at Louise with a surprisingly kindly expression and turned to me.

"Elizabeth and Hugh Mattson, Louise's friends, went to England several months ago," he said, "and when Hugh returned, Elizabeth stayed behind."

"Yes, I heard," I said. "She's visiting with family."

"According to her husband," Louise said and an unaccountable silence descended upon us.

Oh, no, I thought, soon they'll ask me to solve something, forgetting for a moment that no one here knew about my private investigator background. I wasn't about to take this conversation any further.

"Mel is a retired art dealer," Louise said to me. "From New York." Mel glanced at me with the looks of a man who didn't want to be involved in missing persons, either. I decided against mentioning the drifter in the water and my role in retrieving him from certain death.

"Mel, what do you think I should do?" Louise persisted.

"Wait and see. Wait and see," he said.

"But I haven't heard from Hugh Mattson for the longest time and I am always invited to dinner once a week when Elizabeth is at home. And there's a new complication which you probably don't know about. You see, I hear that Hugh has employed what he says is a housekeeper, a young Bajan woman."

And to me she said: "Bajan is what we call ourselves, you know, the people from Barbados. And all I can say is, I don't think she's a housekeeper at all. She's his mistress."

Noelle laughed and Mel shot her a warning look.

"I've heard something to that effect," Mel said. "Given Hugh Mattson's reputation I wouldn't be surprised. But don't you worry, he'll give her marching orders before Elizabeth returns."

He turned to me and changed the subject.

"Have you tried the national dish, the flying fish?"

"No, haven't had a chance yet."

Louise beamed at me. "Did you know that the flying fish use their fins as wings. They shoot right out of the water at a speed of about sixty kilometers an hour."

"I'm amazed."

"They don't really fly, of course, it just seems like it. But they glide through the air and they look as if they do it just for fun."

"Okay," I said, "now that I know so much about them I don't think I'll enjoy eating any. They sound too enterprising to end up on a dinner plate."

"Nonsense," said Mel, "there are thousands of them. But rest assured, we won't serve any tonight."

Louise got up.

"I'm taking Jamie to the plantation this afternoon," she said. "*She* wants to see the place and *I* want to know what's going on."

"It's not hard to guess what's going on, Louise," Noelle said. "Why don't you just leave it alone?"

"Most certainly not," Louise sniffed and flashed her teeth.

"Uh, oh." Mel winked at me. "Watch out. Louise is on the war path."

Louise followed me in her car to the hotel where I parked and switched to hers. Soon we were moving inland on country roads hedged by tall sugar cane which effectively obscured the view around the frequent bends. As we were also on the left side of the road I suddenly found myself concentrating on just hanging on. We swerved right onto a narrower, unpaved road.

"And you are not married, my dear," Louise stated and I thought, oh, God.

While she made a couple of perilous turns which required her attention, my life with Roger flashed before my eyes. We had met in Paris at a party given by one of my fellow students at the Sorbonne and were married three months later to my parents' horror. They had envisioned a smoother transition for me from college to graduate school after my year in Europe and then, eventually, marriage to a suitable young man, just a couple of years older—not twelve, like Roger.

I clutched the dashboard as Louise rushed us around yet another bend in the narrow road. The repressed virgin was a devil at the wheel.

For a while it had felt esoteric to play young matron, returning from boutiques on Rue Faubourg St. Honoré. Clicking my heels on the tiled floors of the little shops selling meats, cheeses, and baguettes. Perusing the vegetable stalls at sidewalk markets. Entertaining Roger's clients. Traveling with Roger. Drinking tea with his mother and her elegant women friends at the Plaza Athénée. Much older, mysteriously busy, dressed by the best Houses, admiring of my French. But chirping at one another above my head, reducing me to childhood. Suffice it to say I divorced Roger four years later and went home to pick up where I'd left off. I'll admit I then floundered a couple of years before I found my niche.

"No, I'm not married," I said to Louise and let it go at that.

We were quite suddenly at the foot of a grand country avenue flanked by wide stretches of grass and tall palm trees. Several flocks of black-belly sheep and red cows grazed peacefully together among the trees. At the end of this splendid entrance way stood a monument of a mansion.

"The Granger-Farley sugar plantation," Louise proclaimed.

CHAPTER 5

The house looked as if it might contain twenty rooms. The exterior was a blend of Tudor and Gothic, the facade made of coral blocks. The windows were arched, the red tiled roof dotted with chimneys. A stone wall surrounded a Spanish style courtyard with the gateway framed by tall columns topped by Greek vases.

"Beautiful, isn't it," Louise said.

I wouldn't put it exactly like that, I thought.

"Quite a mixture of styles," I said.

"Of course, it's a bit run down," Louise continued, "but I tend to see it as it was when I used to come here as a child. You see, Elizabeth's parents took great pride in its maintenance but Hugh Mattson is not a farmer, all he cares about is the sea. He arrived here on a boat from England, met Elizabeth, married her and stayed. Then, when her parents died Hugh naturally had to take over but he has always hired people to do the work and even the planning."

"Any children?" I asked.

"A young daughter," Louise said and looked distractedly at the tangled weeds along the crumbling wall. She led me inside the courtyard which was paved with rough stones. An arched colonnade the length of the building made the entrance door sit in darkness.

Louise didn't bother to knock on the door, just pushed it open and I quickly followed her inside. The interior was dark, too. A few chandeliers hung from the tall ceiling, unlit, and very little light entered through the dusty windows.

I followed Louise into the library which opened up to the left of a staircase. The room was dominated by a large stone-faced fireplace. Above it hung a painting of a plump young woman dressed as a debutante in a white dress, holding a red rose. Not the daughter, I thought, more likely Elizabeth Granger-Farley before she became Mrs. Mattson. A round English face with light brown hair parted in the middle and smoothed down over the ears. A low forehead, a snub nose, and smallish eyes. Pretty because she was young, but no great beauty.

A tall stout man stood behind a huge desk covered with papers. His face was decorated with a handlebar mustache and wild-growing whiskers making him look like a relic from the 19th century. His shirt fit tightly around a cannonball stomach. He was smoking a pipe and had on riding boots. The Squire, I thought.

"Ah, there you are, Louise, got your message," he said. "How good of you to come. And who have we here?"

He looked me over lazily without actually making eye-contact.

"Hugh, I would like you to meet a dear friend of mine, a travel agent from the United States, Jamie Prescott."

I walked across a threadbare Persian rug to shake hands with Hugh Mattson. He was taller than I, and on a good day I measure six feet and a quarter inch. He would have had quite good features if not for his florid complexion and blue-veined nose. Must spend a lot of time in the sun, I decided, unless it was the rum.

"Ah, charmed," he said. "Good of Louise to bring you along." He spoke in a flat tone of voice.

"Sorry to intrude," I said. "I was invited on an impulse to see an actual sugar plantation."

His eyes were pale blue and his hair must have started out blond but was now a mousy gray.

"It'll be my pleasure," he said. A man of few words, I thought.

"Louise tells me your wife is in England," I ventured.

"She's visiting with family."

I looked up.

"A lovely portrait of her," I said.

Mattson didn't look at the painting.

"It was a long time ago."

"Oh, but Elizabeth is still just as lovely," Louise said firmly and moved closer to the fireplace.

"I've never lived on an island," I said. "I'm wondering if, after a while, you feel confined and long for a trip to the continent?"

He suddenly focused on me with more interest.

"That's exactly right," he said. "I'd go bonkers if I didn't get back to Europe every so often."

"Where do you usually go?"

"England, mostly, that's where my wife's family came from. I have no family in England, er, anymore, and only a distant cousin in Denmark on my mother's side. A writer of some kind."

"We have something in common in that case," I said, genuinely surprised. "*My* mother was born in Denmark but I've never been there. How about you?"

"Never been there, either," he said and turned away from me to rustle with some paperwork on his desk. I followed him with a few tentative steps drawn like a magnet to the disorderly piles of papers and books. That's me in a nutshell, I'm a nosey parker. Surely Elizabeth Mattson would have written to her husband and there would be an envelope with her return address. Had I been alone it would have taken me just a few minutes to find one. Then Louise could have compared it with the one she'd written to and been reassured.

But it was not to be. At this point in my silent deliberation, Mattson suddenly grasped my elbow and maneuvered me around Louise towards one of the tall windows.

"You can see some of the plantation from here," he said and squeezed my arm. I freed myself by going closer to the window. Fortunately I found something of interest outside to cover up my move. Unfortunately, he followed me.

"You're looking at the chapel," he said. "It was built by my wife's great-great-grandfather to replace an earlier one."

What I saw was a small building with a pointed roof half obscured by trees.

"Is it still in use?"

"Only for the holidays and special anniversaries. Religion is my wife's hobby."

"Elizabeth loves her chapel." Louise suddenly stood next to me and Mattson let go of my arm. "Come with me and I'll show it to you."

Then the three of us turned around.

The door to the library was flung open and a voice singsang:

"Dahling, ah need your help plenty quick. Upstairs, dahling."

The voice belonged to a tall black woman. She didn't seem in the least taken aback when she saw that "dahling" had company.

"Ahem," said Mattson. "This is my housekeeper, Mirabelle."

"I know you," Louise said. "Don't you work the bar at the cricket club?"

"No, no, no. Ah done change mah job," said Mirabelle. Her nails were long and lacquered blood-red. Not much good for household chores.

"Will you excuse me?" Mattson said to me. His nose had gone a shade more purple. "It seems I am needed elsewhere. Louise will show you around."

And before we could consolidate our new friendship, he was marched off by the tall woman. From behind she looked a lot less regal. Her high rump jiggled as she walked. Mattson stalked away stiffly beside her, his pants sagging around his concave butt. They didn't look back.

CHAPTER 6

"Well, I never," said Louise, her nose appearing more Roman than before. "What an unlovely sight. I am very worried."

And so you should be, I thought.

"She was a bartender, and then some, at the cricket club. That's where Hugh spends time with his sailing cronies. She's up to no good that woman."

"Let's take a look at the chapel," I said. "I doubt if they'll come back downstairs."

We went across the courtyard and turned left around the wall. And there it was, hidden until the very last moment behind a line of trees. The chapel sat like a jewel of coral rock whose tiny irregularities sparkled in the sunlight. The down-scaled windows rose in sharp points. The intricate latticework was painted white, the roof of the chapel covered in red tile, as was the roof of the small vestry at the east side.

A clearing had been made in front of the chapel but grass grew untamed in the ancient cemetery. The names Granger and Farley were there, faintly, on almost all of the lichen-covered stones. The oldest were from the 1750s and the last from the early 1900s. Several stones identified the poor souls only as the "wife of" or the "daughter of," as if those attributes had been their only claim to fame. A few small wreaths resting against the stones had wilted but it was obvious that someone had taken great care in binding them.

The door was heavy and the hinges squeaked but the black iron brackets looked new. I pushed and Louise and I went inside. A musty odor hung about and, yet, there was a cozy feel to the small room. A stone bench built into the wall held several prayer books, and a pair of clogs caked in dried mud lay underneath. A pink wool cardigan hung on a peg on the wall near the door. A couple of gardening tools were stacked neatly in a corner with dried grass still attached.

A narrow trestle table stood against the opposite wall with a basket of wilted flowers—as if put down casually and then forgotten—on its dark-stained, nicked surface. Louise picked up the basket and threw the flowers into a wastebasket.

"When Elizabeth is away no one cares," she said and her nose twitched in disapproval. Then she opened the second door which led into the chapel.

Immediately inside the door stood a stone font on a carved pedestal. The five rows of pews on either side of the aisle were of polished mahogany smooth to the touch. The floor was made of flagstone, large uneven slabs which led to the edge of two steps across the width of the chapel. The altar rose at the back, covered with a white lace cloth on which two tall candelabra flanked a simple cross. The brittle flowers in two low vases were further indication that no one had been here in months. The six narrow windows, three on each side, let in the dimmest of light. The chapel had only one elongated stained-glass window to brighten up the relative gloominess. A white film of dust covered the benches and the altar.

"It needs cleaning," Louise said in a hushed voice. She went behind the altar and re-appeared armed with an enormous cloth.

While Louise dusted I sat down in the front pew and thought of Elizabeth Mattson, nee Granger-Farley, whose sanctuary this was. Why had she decided to stay away for so long? I looked at the well-worn prayer book resting on the shelf in front of me. A small white, lace-edged handkerchief lay next to the book. This must be Elizabeth Mattson's customary place. Suddenly the seat felt inhabited and I moved over one space.

I looked up at the exposed beams which formed the roof of the chapel and slowly a sense of great unease descended upon me. I left the pew abruptly and walked out through the vestry and around the east side of the chapel waved on by Louise who was now removing wilted flowers from the altar.

The graveled path was being taken over by grass and thistles. At the north side I came upon two large slabs of moss green stone covering a pair of identical tombs. The edges were crumbling and one slab was intact while the other had several cracks across. It sat a little askew as if it had been moved at some point and put back carelessly. I looked at the slab more closely and ran my fingers along the underside. It was covered in lichen. The weather-beaten inscriptions had all but vanished but it appeared that at least four ancestors were buried in each tomb. A dried wreath leaned against the one on the far left.

"How exclusive with a private chapel," I said to Louise when she joined me.

"They don't have services any more and they are not allowed to use the cemetery," she said. "But did you know that the great landowners in England usually had private chapels. They brought this tradition with them to Barbados. Life on a farm could go on without interruption if church services for family, and especially for the servants, could take place at any hour on Sunday, and be within walking distance."

We were about to step out from under the shadow of a large tree when Louise put her hand on my arm and squeezed it in warning. The figure of a man appeared around the far corner of the wall. He held his head down furtively and moved rather in the manner of a wolf on the prowl. He never looked our way but bent down close to the ground and picked up a small object which he slipped into his pocket. He turned around and in another second had disappeared the same way he came.

"Well," Louise said vehemently. "I've never liked that chap, I've always felt he was up to no good, and I've told Elizabeth so."

"Who is he?"

"He's Hugh's plantation manager. A Canadian. He's supposed to turn the crops around from sugar cane to vegetables."

"I wonder what he picked up from the ground," I said.

"Up to no good, I tell you," she repeated.

We returned to the car. Louise started it, swung it around, and we crunched down the driveway in a flurry of tiny stone chips. The yellowing sugarcane, interspersed with stretches of ragged banana plants, bent and swayed in the wind on both sides of the narrow, winding lane. We were taking a back road. Dust rose in the air around the car, flew in through the open windows, and we were soon covered in white. I don't mind saying that wheezing and sneezing my way through the rough country-side isn't my idea of relaxation.

Eventually we skidded across jumbles of fleeced sticks strewn along the lane. A truck loaded with sugarcane was just about to move off and four men on top of the shifting load waved to the same man we'd just seen skulking around near the cemetery. He jumped out of a jeep and I wondered how he'd managed to get out here ahead of us. He went to the truck and spoke briefly to the four men. Then he waved to us. Louise stopped the car and waited for him to approach.

"How are you today, Mrs. Higginbotham," he said to Louise but he was looking at me.

And I looked back into warm brown eyes, and saw white teeth and full lips surrounded by a short, curly black beard. It's Roger all over again, I thought. My heart had thumped unexpectedly and I couldn't believe the Pavlovian reaction.

"I am fine, thank you. Jamie, this is Hugh's plantation manager, Jean-Pierre François. Jamie Prescott is a travel agent from the States," said Louise. "We have just come from the chapel."

Jean-Pierre looked up at her sharply. Then he smiled.

"I was at the house talking to Hugh just now. I must have missed you," he said to Louise. And to me: "On vacation?"

"Just arrived," I said.

"Let me guess, you're at the best hotel on the island?"

"I certainly hope so."

He leaned in through the window and handed me a huge wooden stick of sugarcane.

"Try it," he said. "It's very sweet."

It looked like firewood and I shook my head.

"Thanks a lot but I'd just as soon keep my teeth."

He laughed, sunk his own teeth into the sugar cane and bit off a huge sliver, sucked out the juice and spat out the remains.

"Messy business," I said and looked across the field. "Did you find what you were looking for on the ground back at the house?"

I heard Louise suck in her breath through the gap between her front teeth.

"*Pardon?*" Jean-Pierre took a step back.

"Yes, pardon my curiosity."

He looked me straight in the eye and said: "I do not know what you are talking about."

"Oh, okay. What are the men doing out there?"

"Harvesting." His tone of voice was dismissive. "The trucks will take the cane to the sugar mill. This plantation has its own. It even has one of the old wind-mills, it's been restored but hasn't been in use for over a hundred years."

"It would be interesting to see the actual process," I said more to Louise than to Jean-Pierre.

"I can tell you how it works," Louise said. "The cane is crushed and the juice extracted. The stalks are then dried and used for fuel. The juice is strained and clarified, then boiled. That's when the sugar crystalizes. Rum is made from the waste matter left over from the production of sugar and molasses."

A group of hefty women in cotton frocks and aprons passed us without looking up, intent on keeping the balance of the enormous green buckets perched on their heads. Their thick arms lay across their stomachs, their work-worn hands folded. They were heading towards a group of small, wiry boys hacking away at the cane with huge machetes. They looked no more than eight years old.

Louise turned the key in the ignition.

Jean-Pierre stood back and I noticed he didn't wear sunglasses which would account for the sun-streaked laugh lines around his eyes.

"Aren't you the devil." Louise winked at me. "Didn't pick up anything from the ground. Hah. I tell you he's no good. And he has a bad reputation with the ladies."

I let her last remark go. I don't need a baby sitter but I did wonder what he'd been doing outside the wall. Obviously something he didn't want to discuss. None of your business, I reminded myself.

The lane wound around the field and the sugar mill appeared at the far end. A huge crane swung around and scooped up the cane which had been dumped there from the trucks. We continued along the edge of the field, bumping up and down on the uneven terrain. The dust settled in my hair and gritted between my teeth.

When Louise dropped me off at the hotel around three, she looked tired.

"My dear," she said. "I hope you don't mind awfully but I think I'll beg off going out to dinner tonight. You go ahead and have fun with Noelle and Mel. I'll call to offer my regrets. But why don't you come to town the day after tomorrow and we'll have lunch at the cricket club."

"Love to," I said not quite truthfully.

I still had time for a swim.

CHAPTER 7

I slathered on a liberal coat of sun screen, 45 SPF. That should give me just enough color to convince myself, once back home, that I'd been to the Caribbean.

Then I put on the turquoise and purple bikini to go with my still pale skin, stuck my feet into flip-flops and stepped down from the porch. The ground outside the cottage was covered with glossy, green leaves rustled by tiny critters flitting swiftly across the path leading to the beach. I walked the dozen or so steps to the edge of the garden where the semi-darkness of the damp enclosure gave way to the bright reflection of the sea.

I sat down in my beach chair under the umbrella, put on my sunglasses, and told the waiter to bring me a rum punch.

The air carried a sharp tang of water and seaweed. Several children were playing beach cricket and I watched them lazily as they swung at a wicket—made of four sticks of driftwood—near the water's edge. I closed my eyes and the distant sounds suddenly triggered memories of childhood playgrounds where the hum of other kids' voices had conjured up wishful images of summer.

When I looked up a shadow had fallen across my legs. Jean-Pierre François towered above me.

"May I?" he said and dragged a lounge chair over next to mine.

"How did you find me?" I know I sounded annoyed. I don't like being taken by surprise.

"There's only one 'best' hotel in Barbados," he said. He motioned to the waiter and ordered a rum punch. The waiter looked at me questioningly and I nodded a silent 'yes, put it on my tab.' They don't handle cash orders on the beach.

Jean-Pierre sat down and, in the process, quickly scanned the ring finger of my left hand.

"How long are you staying," he said.

"Oh, haven't quite decided yet." I was purposefully evasive.

"You're a biker?"

"How do you figure that?"

"I saw the bike on your porch. Are you planning a biking tour of the island?"

I looked at him, irritated.

"And how long have *you* been here?" I said.

"Eight months. I'm supposed to turn their farming methods around."

"I understand Mrs. Mattson has been away in England for several months. Do people usually travel to Europe for that long?"

"*Bièn sûr.* I think it is not unusual. They do that if they have the money. I think they get stir-crazy living on such a small island."

"What's she like?"

"She gets on everybody's nerves with her religion. And she isn't interested in sailing which is what Hugh Mattson is passionate about."

"And the daughter?"

Jean-Pierre sat up in his chair and put down his glass.

"What *about* the daughter?"

"I just wondered if she sails with her father or stays home with her mother? How old is she?"

"I have no idea."

"Well, is she a child or a grown-up?"

"*Eh, bién.* I guess she's a grown-up."

I finished the last of my rum punch but kept the ice in my mouth.

"If you'll excuse me I'm going for a swim," I said and got up.

He jumped up as if ready to follow me but when I didn't extend an invitation he remained standing. When I got to the water's edge I turned around and saw him disappear up the hill towards the hotel.

I swam a good bit out. When the water turned cold under my feet, I started a fast crawl parallel to the beach. I stopped swimming to float on my back and realized I had covered a distance much greater than the first time when I had swum only as far as the two fishing boats. Now they were gone. On the beach I observed several groups of young guys with matted hair under cone-shaped knit hats, and small enclaves of teenage girls. A short distance further down the beach a coral rock—at least ten feet tall—stood glinting like a full moon. I decided to take a brisk walk to observe it up close.

The wind blew somewhat harder than what I usually like, but you can't have everything. The stone was much larger than it had appeared from a distance, at least fifteen feet tall and as many wide. The surface was deeply crenelated, a zig-zag maze secreted by millions of tiny polyps to support their distant lives. Scattered across were deeper holes, dug as if by especially enterprising polyps.

I touched the surface gingerly—it was sharp as needles. I walked around the stone and stood a few moments studying it with the sun at my back. The low rays shining on the coral brought out a myriad of colors and made the surface of the rock sparkle like sapphires.

That's when I saw him. He walked towards me looking down at his feet as if searching for gold. The tattoo on his arm, I now saw, extended all the way across his shoulders. He was no more attractive today than he'd been when I dragged him out of the water.

He walked about thirty feet to my right and after he'd passed me I followed him. He was still paying close attention to the sand beneath his feet, never looked up, never looked back, an easy target to follow. He veered down closer to the water's edge and I gained on him until I was within talking distance.

A small speedboat ran noisily alongside us and I was just starting to get annoyed at the intrusion when it suddenly soared towards the beach, pulled up sharply, and two black men jumped out. My tattooed friend froze for one second. Then he turned almost into my arms, veered around me, and ran. And I don't mean just ran. He flew. The fear I'd seen in his face must have jump-started his adrenaline.

The two men had to traverse several feet of water before reaching the shore and this impediment gave Tattoo a slight advantage. I decided to give him some help.

I jumped up and down in place as if exercising and when the two reached me I bumped into the first one who tripped and lost his balance. The second man tried to avoid us but my foot was in his way and he fell. I turned in my tracks and did a 1K sprint back to the coral rock. They followed me but sprinting didn't seem to be their best sport and I got there way before them.

By the time I reached the rock, Tattoo had disappeared into a large group of guys on the beach. His pursuers reached me and circled around me a couple of times. They looked me over carefully as if to remember me well, and I did the same. They didn't touch me although they looked as if they would have liked nothing better. They walked rather than sprinted back to their boat.

I was catching my breath behind the coral rock when I saw Jean-Pierre. He stood a short distance away, hands hanging at his sides, rooted to the ground, watching two people, a man and a woman, scuffling on the beach. I could hear their voices faintly above the rush of water being whipped up by the wind.

The woman kicked at the man's legs and scratched at his face while he had a good grip on her hair. I couldn't believe it. It was Tattoo. He seemed to have run from one skirmish into another. Somehow she now managed to twist out of his hand and, abruptly, the fight stopped. Tattoo turned his back, walked away from her up the slope from the beach and was gone.

And she—she came floating across the sand towards Jean-Pierre. As if nothing at all had happened. A juicy young thing in a minuscule black tanga which barely disguised her crotch—and otherwise topless.

Jean-Pierre took a step back but she continued to move towards him until she was close enough to put her hands on his shoulders and let them glide down his arms. She spread his fingers apart and intertwined them with her own. She lifted her face to his and brushed her breasts against him. They were tanned the even color of her body.

Jean-Pierre stepped back but not fast enough. She followed him. He wrenched his hands free but she let her's drop and ran them around his butt and down his thighs in a swift caress. He pushed her away, shouted, and she seemed to loose her spunk.

That's when I stepped out from behind the coral rock.

"Hi, again," I said to him.

Jean-Pierre looked stupefied and the juicy thing got back some of her spunk. She glared from Jean-Pierre to me and back again.

"Who is *she*?" she said.

I remained motionless, adjusted the straps of my bikini top and, looking at her streamlined body, felt absurdly glad that I hadn't let mine go. My abs could compete with the best.

"Well," she said.

Jean-Pierre's face had lost most of its color.

"Jamie Prescott," he said. "Meet Amaryllis Mattson."

CHAPTER 8

"Amaryllis," Noelle snorted. "Nymphomaniac. The island whore."

"You're a little hard on her, aren't you? All you women are." Mel Kramer lowered the hoods over his eyes and winked at me. "It wouldn't be a touch of jealousy, would it?"

Noelle, in diaphanous harem pants gathered at the ankles, a tight-fitting top showing a slice of brown midriff, and silver sandals, didn't look as if she had to be jealous of any nymphomaniac. She ignored him. They're like an old, married couple, I thought, talking above each other's heads. Mel looked bored.

We were sitting on white wicker peacock chairs at a round dining table. Outside the sliding doors fireflies moved in silver clouds along a brick wall at the back of the patio. Mendelsohn's Violin Concerto in E minor played in the background.

"Amaryllis has slept her way through white and black Barbados, assorted tourists, and transients. What's to be jealous of?" Noelle looked bored, too, as if this subject had already been discussed to tears.

Noelle's house—or was it Mel's? I hadn't quite figured it out—had been a revelation. The surrounding buildings were plain little chattel houses with white trim, humble in the extreme, painted in pastel colors, or not painted at all. Louise Higginbotham had already told me about the original slave houses—loo and water out back—built to be disassembled and rebuilt whenever their hapless owners were forced to move to a different plantation.

That's how the house had looked from the front, except for a small porch with Victorian curlicues and white wicker furniture. A fat ginger cat on the railing had greeted me with startling green eyes. The front-door hinges squeaked and Noelle, standing in the frame, had let me into Aladdin's cave.

Now I looked around. The walls were hung with embroidered tapestries in deep red, gold, and black. Throw-rugs were scattered across the wooden floor amongst low divans and tasseled pillows. The two front rooms were illuminated by flickering candles in burnished brass lamps swinging in the draft from the louvered windows. It was simultaneously enticing and claustrophobic. I had a sudden craving for my minimalist house in Bethesda where each chair, each table, each painting occupied its own serene space.

Mel was at a sideboard crammed with a variety of rum bottles and juices. A line of glasses stood ready to be filled. He splashed a bit from this bottle, and a bit from that, into a stainless container, gave the transparent top cover a smart rap and began to shake it. He turned to me and grinned.

"Ask anyone around here and they'll tell you I mix the best damn rum punch on the island."

"I believe you."

"You can't mix whiskies. But rum, that's another matter. After much experimentation I've arrived at what is now known as 'Mel's Concoction.' Three ounces of Light, three of Gold, three of Extra Old Dark, a splash of Grand Marnier, water, sugar, lime and tangerine juice, and *Presto!* Your rum punch over crushed ice."

I got up, stretched, and walked around the room looking at the wall tapestries.

"Here," said Mel, "your glass."

And I turned to him just as he pushed a drawer shut with his hip. It was deftly done but I had glimpsed the handgun and the two clips.

Mel handed me the glass with a flourish and before long my eyeballs were rotating.

"Amaryllis," I said through the blur. "Blooms gloriously—once—and then what's left? An eternity of boring, lank leaves."

Her face had been a reflection of her mother's in the painting above the fireplace. Low forehead, squirrel cheeks, snub nose. But it had a vitality the painting lacked. Full, red lips and white, white teeth set off by a spectacular tan. And that, I had to admit, with her spiked, bleached hair and young lean body, was electrifying.

"Not worth the trouble. Give it too much water and the bulb rots. I say, toss the whole thing out." Noelle raised her glass and we grinned at each other.

"Women!" Mel got up. "Flowers," he muttered to himself and disappeared into the kitchen while Noelle made no signs of getting up. After much scrambling with pots and pans he returned with a huge seafood salad, bread, and wine.

"Ummmh," I said and sunk my teeth into the crusty baguette. "Do me a favor, explain this business about 'good day,' 'good evening,' and 'good night'?"

"Simple," said Mel. "It's 'good day' until 1 p.m., 'good evening' until six, and 'good night' until it's 'good day' in the morning.

"You call that simple?"

"Not really, but you know what they say: When in Rome . . ."

After dinner Noelle motioned me to follow her down a narrow hall lit by live candles in wrought iron holders on the walls. A hazardous detail in a wooden house, I thought. The candles flickered ominously in the draft created when we passed.

Noelle pushed open the door to her bedroom and left me standing there, gaping. No more Aladdin's cave. We were now in La-la-land. The room was white-carpeted with a pink, circular bed piled high with frilly, chintzy pillows, and a quilted headboard sparkling with tiny beads. Above the bed hung a painting in tones of peach, yellow, and pink, of two figures in voluptuous coupling.

Surely not, I thought and looked up at the ceiling. But sure enough. A large round mirror strategically placed above the bed. This must be what kept Mel retired in Barbados. To dispel some wholly unsuitable images from flooding my mind, I stepped inside.

"Where did you get all this? Somehow I can't imagine it on display in a staid Barbados furniture store."

"Made to order." Noelle went to a walk-in closet where I glimpsed rows of colorful garments and just as many shoes. "I got your painting. And two more—but please do not feel obligated. We keep a few of our favorites at home for special customers. Would you like to see them?"

Ten minutes later I was the new owner of three Prèfête Duffaut paintings. The cerulean blue water set off the reds, greens, and yellows of houses clinging to imaginary mountain sides. Quarter-inch immaculate figures in straw hats strolled on the beach, and hurried up the narrow roads. Duffaut's leitmotifs. Museum quality and worth a small fortune. Which I paid.

Having presumably abandoned the dirty dishes in the kitchen, Mel was lying on a low divan, legs elevated on a stack of pillows. Holding a glass of his own concoction on his chest, and with eyes half closed, his feet moved to the insistent strains of Ravel.

Noelle placed a bowl of hibiscus on the empty dining table and I sat down across from Mel in one of two massive, dark-stained wooden armchairs—early English, I guessed. My feet dangled several inches from the floor and I pulled them up under me, leaving my sandals behind. My hand swept down over the armrest and I was rewarded with a gentle sniff from the ginger cat before she arched upward and landed on my lap. She circled around on nimble feet before settling down, purring. She squinted at me briefly with those emerald eyes.

Noelle brought me another glass of wine and sat down in the second English chair. Large as she was, the chair with its high crested back, joined legs and deep seat, made her seem almost tiny. We sat in silence for several minutes and listened to Mel's music.

"Tell me what you know about the Mattsons." I had to raise my voice to be heard above Ravel.

"*He's* a creep. *She's* pathetic. The *daughter* is a whore."

"That much I've gathered. You've known them, what, three, four years? Do they travel to England every year? And does Elizabeth always stay there and he returns alone?"

"*Bién*. They do go every year and she usually stays there longer than he."

"Why do you find her pathetic?" I said.

"*Ah, mà chérie*, she is the doormat type." Noelle took a contemptuous sip of her drink. "Repressed in that particular British way. On your back and think of England. *En fin*, I can't really blame Hugh Mattson."

"Hmm. And what about him?"

"He's bedded most of the low-life women in Barbados. Get's them on his boat and takes off every weekend. *Alors*, a beautiful boat. Outfitted to the hilt."

"Wait a minute. You've gone sailing with him?"

"Just that once when I first came here and before I knew anything about him." Noelle didn't look embarrassed in the least. "Met him at the cricket club and fell for his line. He was a lot slimmer then and not bad looking except for that nose. Hideous."

"Not to mention the handlebar mustache and those wild whiskers." We giggled and Mel sent us an exasperated look. Then we sipped our drinks in silence.

"And the women," Noelle said after a while. "Elizabeth and Louise run around in tweed skirts, woollen cardigans, and flat shoes, in the middle of summer. Too British for words and they're third or fourth generation here."

"But Elizabeth has money," Mel said and looked up from his music. "And Hugh can't touch it."

"How do you know that?" I said.

"Everyone knows. This is such a small place."

"And Amaryllis? Does she have money?"

"Oh, her." Noelle laughed. "Don't worry about her, there's a trust fund for her. Of course, she's rather like Prince Charles, she'll have to wait until her mother throws in the towel. In the meantime, she must behave in order to get her allowance."

"Doesn't she have a job?"

"A job? *Mais non,* don't be ridiculous. She's much too busy to hold down a job."

Mel had gone back to his music and Noelle and I stopped talking until the CD finished.

"Ah." He tilted his glass and spilled liquid down his shirt front. "Oh, shit." He brushed the drops off but didn't get up. "So, are you enjoying it here, so far?" he said to me.

"Yes, and no," I said, and I suppose it was the rum concoction that spoke. "I had a weird experience almost the minute I arrived. I've been trying to forget it because I'm rather obsessed with having a peaceful vacation."

"What happened?" Mel said, and I told them about my find in the sea, the subsequent rescue.

"Drugged-out drifters," he exclaimed, and Noelle looked at me strangely.

"*Mon Dieu,*" she said. "You're a hero. And did he thank you?"

"As a matter of fact, he didn't, but it's not a thank you I'm after," I said. "It's a vacation."

"In that case you ought to see the other face of Barbados." Mel's voice dropped in facetious menace. "The rugged east coast."

"I'm planning to. I'm going biking across the island in a couple of days."

"Now, there's an idea. I should get my wheels dusted off and accompany you." Mel looked as if he would need to do quite a bit of dusting before he was ready for a fifty mile ride.

"Don't be silly, *mon amour*," Noelle said and looked at him with a tiny smile. "You're in no condition to go biking."

"I need a new hobby," he said, looking sour.

"But before you find one, you must concentrate on our garden party."

"You will come, of course," Mel said to me, still looking bored. "There's going to be an interesting variety of people, friends of mine from New York, friends of ours from here."

I accepted the invitation and wondered how much longer he planned to stay retired in Barbados. Noelle—and her circular bed—must be the closest to exotic he'd find here.

We listened to a few more CDs and then I left. I got back to the hotel at ten. I took my three new paintings—stretched on binder frames—propped one on the back of the sofa, one on the armchair, and the third on the floor. I sat down and admired my acquisitions imagining them on my walls in Bethesda. And, somehow, I had the elusive Archibald Brewster looking at them with me.

All the while I wondered why Mel Kramer needed a gun.

CHAPTER 9

Schools of hungry sergeant-majors and yellowtail snappers crowded around me for the breadcrumbs I hadn't thought of bringing. Squid, sting rays, and eels drifted by without paying attention. The coral reef teemed with life. A truly wonderful underwater world.

I carefully breathed in the compressed air from the yellow tank strapped around my shoulders and waist. I thanked heaven for my healthy lungs and clear sinus cavities even though the bottom depth here was only about forty feet and the top of the reef about twenty feet under the water's surface. The perfect spot, my divemaster, Beth, had said, and she was right.

Beth now swam into my field of vision and motioned me to follow her down and around to a reef with spectacular walls and pinnacles. She shone her powerful beam and the coral sprang to life in oranges, whites, yellows, blues, and purples. Mussels and anemones clung to the pristine reef, and in a dramatic swim-through a cascade of fish opened like a curtain in front of me. Following closely behind Beth I moved my feet languidly in order to find the elusive seahorses and frogfish. Instead, what I swam around was a small metal casket wedged in between two reefs. I swam around it several times until Beth signed for me to ascend. I followed her up in a straight line. After we surfaced together we climbed into the speedboat which took us back to the beach.

I sat there with my face to the sun, and felt my suntan improve and my equilibrium stabilize while I thought disapprovingly of the debris people threw overboard. This was my first morning of scuba-diving and I was regretting having agreed to meet Louise Higginbotham for lunch in Bridgetown but it couldn't be helped now.

I watched idly as scores of sailboats bobbed up and down close to shore. One boat pulled at anchor further out.

"Nice yacht," I said to Beth who had plunked herself down next to me.

"Oh, that one. Belongs to one of the big shots around the marina."

We watched together as several people moved around on the jetty. One man dressed all in white stood out and I recognized the tall figure of Hugh Mattson. I got up and sauntered down towards him. He didn't notice me until I said hello.

"How d'you do." He didn't look especially pleased to see me and didn't bother to pretend.

A speedboat roared up to the jetty and two men jumped out. I watched them load enough provisions to last a week.

"Going away for a while?" I shouted to Mattson above the wind.

He must have heard me but he didn't bother to answer. He just looked right through me or, rather, over my left shoulder scanning the beach quickly. I turned around automatically but saw nothing of significance. Just practically nude bodies on beach towels. When I looked back at Mattson he had stepped away and was halfway into the boat which the men had finished loading. Without another look at me, he gave an order and they sped away.

I returned to the diveshop after this rude dismissal, looked around for Beth, picked up my gear when I didn't see her, and walked to the parking lot. I stopped when I heard the roar of a speedboat and watched it pull up to the jetty. I looked through the clearing between the trees. A lone figure ambled leisurely towards the boat and I felt a jolt of surprise.

It was Noelle.

She was dressed in a flowing white skirt and a tank-top. She stopped just before stepping onto the jetty, groped in her handbag, put a phone to her ear and listened. I saw her hesitate, look around briefly—probably seeing the same view of sunbathers that I'd observed minutes before—drop the phone back in her bag, and jump into the boat. It flew away towards Mattson's yacht.

I wondered if Mel Kramer knew of this but told myself it was none of my business. Still, I answered myself, I'll find out.

By one o'clock I was in Bridgetown to join Louise Higginbotham for lunch. She was at her desk listening to a woman and a man who sat at the edge of their chairs, leaning forward earnestly. I sat down and waited but not out of earshot or eyesight. As Bob Makowski likes to say, I have laser eyesight and 20/20 hearing. Translation: I read upside down and listen in on other people's conversations. Topsy likes to say I'm just plain nosy.

They apparently were Mr. and Mrs. Harris—and so obviously British. The first thing I noticed about the woman was bare feet in enormous unfashionable sandals. Then my laser eyes traveled up and took in a 1960s-style flowery dress, and lank gray hair resting on sloping shoulders. Her husband wore a pair of similar sandals but had on black wool socks. His pants and short-sleeved shirt looked as if he'd slept in them. He peered at Louise from under a shapeless canvas hat.

I looked at the two small suitcases on the floor next to their chairs and wondered why they'd come to Barbados. They didn't look prepared for a leisurely vacation.

"We 'aven't 'eard from 'im at all in several months. That's why we're 'ere," the man said.

"We're ever so worried about 'im. We saw your sign and thought you could 'elp us find some affordable lodgings," the woman added.

Louise made a couple of phone calls before scribbling down an address on a piece of paper.

"You can catch a bus on the next corner and tell the driver you need to get off just before Prospect Bay. It's a Bed & Breakfast. Thirty Barbados dollars a night. The cheapest you'll find."

"'ow much is the fare?" Mr. Harris pulled out a handful of Bajan coins from a worn pocket and held them out for Louise to inspect. She picked a few and said, "This should do it. They like to get exact change."

With many ta's ever so much the Harrises left for the bus with their small suitcases.

"Looking for their son, Andy," Louise said and shook her head. "They shouldn't have wasted their money. These young students come, over-stay, and eventually find their way home again."

"Yes, it seems a bit extreme for parents to traipse all this way in pursuit."

As promised, Louise took me to the cricket club for lunch. Housed at the edge of the cricket field in a low building reminiscent of stables the entrance smelled of sweaty bodies and wet towels. In contrast, the dining room where rattan tables were set with green and white tablecloths felt very Caribbean. The trade winds blew in through the open windows and flicked across our faces.

My hopes that flying fish would not be on the menu were quickly rewarded. Instead, it looked like soggy veggies and roast beef. Louise had her mineral water and I nursed a glass of white wine.

"And have you heard anything from your friend, Elizabeth, yet?" I asked and was immediately sorry because

Louise put down her fork and knife and leaned across the table with a determined expression in her fierce blue eyes. Her high-bridged nose quivered.

"It really is the limit," she said. "I called Hugh the other day after I left you. He was not only rude and said he'd had a letter from Elizabeth just a few days ago and that she's fine, but he as good as told me to stop calling him and that if Elizabeth doesn't want to write to me there's nothing he can do about it."

I had to admit to myself that apart from the rudeness he might have something of a point.

"Tell me a little bit about her," I said. The image of Louise and her friend Elizabeth—dressed in woollen cardigans and walking shoes all through summer—flashed through my mind. Louise was wearing them now.

"She's quite amazing." Louise picked up her fork and knife and resumed eating. "Her charitable organization is a big part of her life, it has become her full time job just as the travel agency is mine. She is a fund-raiser second-to-none."

There you go, I thought, a new picture emerging and strangely different from the one Noelle had painted of Elizabeth. I was confused. Which was it to be? Meek and pathetic, or clever and resilient?

"And does she, herself, contribute?" I said.

"Yes, of course, my dear, that's how it all started. With Elizabeth helping a few poor farm families on the plantation out of her own trust fund. But for the last ten years, at least, the organization has raised much more."

"And her husband? Is he involved in charitable work as well?"

"Hugh?" Louise's disdainful voice told volumes. "Certainly not. He doesn't have money. And whenever he opens his mouth it is to ridicule Elizabeth. He scoffs at her charitable work, he mocks her religion."

"They don't appear to have much in common. He seems to be more of a sailing enthusiast. I happened to see him this morning boarding his boat at the marina near Holetown." I decided not to mention Noelle.

"Indeed, that's all he does. Sail. But thank goodness, Elizabeth won't let him sink any of *her* money into the bigger yacht he covets."

"She never goes sailing with him?"

"It may seem strange to you to find two islanders who do not love the sea. Elizabeth and I enjoy people and flowers, but we want solid ground under our feet. I never learned how to swim and Elizabeth didn't, either." Louise pushed her plate aside and laughed. "But here we go talking about me. What about you, my dear? Are you having some fun?"

Fun? Not quite yet, I thought.

"I'm beginning to relax," I said. And for want of something else to say I made the mistake of telling her about my recent experiences in Peru, how some fast work by Interpol in Paris had helped me solve the case when a woman in the tour group I had taken to Machu Picchu was murdered.

Louise listened avidly but at the end of my narration was focused only on the fact that in addition to being a travel agent I was also a private investigator. I told her about my work for Bob Makowski and about some of the cases I've investigated.

"And you've found many missing persons, have you?" She lifted those eyebrows and peered at me sideways. "How do you go about it?"

Ah, I thought, how do I go about it. Today, if people are very determined they can disappear quite effectively. There are ways of obtaining false birth certificates, social security numbers, driver's licences, and credit cards. If people are missing through no fault of their own, the trail becomes just as complicated.

"How do you go about it?" Louise repeated. "For example, could you find Elizabeth in England for me?"

"Well, now," I laughed, somewhat startled. "You could probably do that yourself. All you need to do is find out the return address on the envelopes Elizabeth has sent to Hugh and check if it's the one he gave you. On the other hand, it could be that she's too busy to write."

Louise looked doubtful.

"The thing is," I insisted, "your letter was not returned with a notation 'unknown at this address,' or 'not deliverable,' or however the phrase goes in England."

"No, my letter wasn't returned. But the postal service isn't what it used to be." Louise looked at me with purpose. "I know I'm imposing on you but I need to find out. Will you help me?"

I thought of Hugh Mattson's overflowing desk in the library at the plantation. Surely it would be only a matter of a few uninterrupted moments to find an envelope from England. And Hugh was away, sailing.

Against my better judgment, I agreed.

CHAPTER 10

"I've called the house," Louise said when we were on the road the next day. "No one is home. You saw Hugh take off on his boat and Amaryllis is on the beach all day."

"And what if she isn't?"

"If her car—it's a small red MG—is parked at the gate we will know. Then I will think of something."

We were going at a heady forty miles per hour and Louise looked strangely excited. The qualms I'd had last night about the trip were intensifying but, I thought, this won't take long and then I'll spend the rest of the afternoon on the beach.

"And what about the plantation manager," I said. "He seems to be around the house all the time?"

"I'll soon get rid of him."

I had come to a full stop behind a bus and Louise dug into her roomy handbag.

"Here," she said, "this is the postcard Elizabeth sent me three months ago."

I looked at a picture of an idyllic village scene and turned it around to the back. The stamp had fallen off and the card was written in purple ink in a round school-girlish hand.

'See you soon, dear Louise,' it said and was signed Elizabeth with a flourish.

"Elizabeth always uses purple ink," Louise said.

The road stretched before us long and narrow. The air shimmered in the sunlight and I strained to anticipate anything coming around the bends of the narrow road, an entirely useless task. Whenever a car came seemingly out of nowhere obscured by the tall sugarcane hedges, I was taken completely by surprise.

After we took a right turn from the highway and went down the winding lane past the sugar mill I thought I saw Jean-Pierre's jeep parked at the side but he, himself, wasn't there. A few minutes later we turned down the tree-lined avenue towards the plantation house. There were no cars parked in front of the gate.

"Amaryllis is not at home," Louise said and directed me around to the left where I parked the car close to the wall well behind some unruly shrubs.

"There," she said with satisfaction in her voice. "Now we can't be seen."

Okay, I thought, let's get this over with. The entire scheme now seemed absurdly paranoid to me.

We walked through the gate, down the flagstone path and up to the front door. As before, Louise didn't bother to knock and, as before, the door was unlocked. We stood for a moment in the foyer listening to the silence. Through the open door to the library I could see the painting of Elizabeth over the fireplace and in the semi-darkness her eyes—and her hand resting just above her heart—seemed to speak of hidden pain. I was caught up in the atmosphere of undefined intrigue and forgot about my earlier misgivings. I moved quickly towards the library.

"You stand guard," I said to Louise. "I'll do the searching."

Louise readily agreed.

"If anyone comes in," she said, "I'll say you've gone to the bathroom."

"Where's the bathroom?"

"It's through the library, the door at the back. Then first door on your right in the corridor."

I left Louise in the foyer, closed the door to the library behind me and set to work. Hugh Mattson's desk was still in the same unbelievable disorder as when I last saw it, and I was here to sort through it. With my usual deft touch, of course.

I started from the left-hand side of the desk and worked my way to the right. A green shaded table lamp stood in the midst of a pile of bills which I sifted through quickly. I was looking for an envelope with English stamps, or a card, or a sheet of paper in Elizabeth's purple handwriting. The next pile was a sheaf of statements from Barclays Bank and another batch from the Barbados National Bank. There were bills from the electric company and from an earth-moving contractor, newsletters from the cricket club, and old copies of the *Nation* and the *Advocate*. Next to these I found an envelope with travel information about England with a notation on the cover written in purple ink. I had no time to take a closer look. Clutching the envelope I quickly riffled through the rest of the desk, picking up a book with a bright red cover to examine a pile of letters underneath it.

That's when the door opened and Louise scuttled inside. I flung the book back on the desk but stayed with the envelope while turning to Louise.

"Someone's coming." She looked petrified and apparently her plans for diverting attention and get rid of the 'someone' had evaporated. I grabbed her by the arm and hustled her out the back door into the narrow corridor. She clung to me and looked as if she was about to pass out.

I shook her by the shoulders and her face took on a green hue.

"Stop that," I hissed and stuffed the envelope into her large handbag, out of sight. I left her leaning against the wall while I went back to the door to the library which had been left ajar. I peeked through and saw nothing but heard two voices. Jean-Pierre and a woman's. I widened the gap in the door and, as expected, saw Amaryllis.

The voices faded and I saw them move towards the windows. The words came to me as if filtered through cotton wool.

"I . . . you," Amaryllis said.

"I want . . ." Jean-Pierre sounded hoarse.

"Well, you can't . . . now, can you? She has a . . . on you just as she's always . . . me."

"It's up to . . . now, or is he all talk and no action?"

"Don't worry, he's taking care . . . ."

And that's when Louise sneezed. Not just a genteel, suppressed sound but a gigantic explosion. The conversation in the library stopped abruptly and I heard hurried steps on the wooden floor.

"Who's there?" Amaryllis said.

I grabbed Louise by the arm, opened the door briskly, and entered the library prepared to give my performance with or without assistance from Louise.

"*You!*" Amaryllis shouted at me. "What are *you* doing in my house." She turned to stare at Jean-Pierre who in turn stared at *me*.

Louise pulled out her inevitable handkerchief and blew into it with the same force which had produced her sneeze. She wiped the tip of her nose with a curiously reddish effect and through this diversionary tactic got herself under control.

"Don't be rude, dear," she said to Amaryllis in a firm schoolmistress kind of voice. "Your mother would be appalled. Jamie is a friend of mine. You apologize to her, you hear."

"Sorry, Aunt Louise." Amaryllis managed to avoid looking at me. "What are you doing here?"

"I needed the comfort of your bathroom, my dear. Jamie is a travel agent from the States and I'm taking her across island to show her Harrison's Cave and the Flower Forest and everything else she'll want to include in the tours she's planning for next year."

Amaryllis stared at me. Her spiked hair was no longer yellow. It was dyed flaming red.

Louise, in her wool cardigan and flat shoes, her handbag over her arm in the manner of the queen on a visit to one of her humble subjects, trained her blue eyes on Amaryllis across the expanse of her nose, ignored Jean-Pierre who apparently had lost his power of speech, and proceeded towards the exit.

"You get on with whatever you were doing, my dear," Louise said, "we won't keep you any longer."

I smiled my best travel agent smile and followed Louise out the door leaving Amaryllis and Jean-Pierre in the middle of the floor, staring.

We hurried down the steps, down the path, out the gate and around the wall to the car. I maneuvered back and forth to get the back fender disengaged from the shrubbery and we were on our way along the wide avenue. The red cows and the black-bellied sheep were chewing philosophically and never even looked up as we passed.

"I'm impressed," I said. "You managed that well."

"I actually enjoyed it." Louise whinnied. "But tell me, did you find anything on Hugh's desk?" I had expected her to comment on the conversation in the library between Amaryllis and Jean-Pierre but now realized that only I had heard it. I decided to keep it to myself until I could digest its meaning.

"It's in your handbag, and I don't think it's of any use to you," I said. "Just a folder with travel brochures to England. It was the only thing with purple ink."

"You didn't see any letters or cards from Elizabeth, then?"

"No, I didn't. But that doesn't mean she hasn't sent any. It only means that he didn't leave them lying around."

I didn't say it but Louise seemed to accept the fact that she was at a dead end. She wet her protruding teeth and cast an imperial glance my way.

"My dear," she said, "it is such a pity that Elizabeth and Amaryllis can't share more mother-daughter moments. There's the age gap, of course. No one thought Elizabeth would ever get married. She was thirty-seven when she met Hugh and almost forty when Amaryllis was born and Elizabeth was never good at handling her. Amaryllis is rather wild. Loves everything to do with the sea. Sailing, swimming, diving, surfing. And Elizabeth, I am sorry to say, is deathly afraid of the water."

"Yes, from your descriptions of Elizabeth and my knowledge, although slight, of Amaryllis, I can't say I'm surprised they've had trouble."

We were now out on the main road.

"Let us go to the caves," she said. "We might as well do something constructive with our afternoon."

I'll take a swim tonight in the moonlight instead, I thought. And who knew, maybe I ought to make Louise's assertion to Amaryllis come true. Topsy and I probably should have scuba-diving tours to Barbados on our program and it seemed a waste of opportunity for me not to look at the tourist attractions with a professional eye to the future. My relaxing vacation was turning into the proverbial busman's holiday.

The caves were more dramatic than I had imagined with stalactites and stalagmites hanging down from the ceilings and pushing up from the floors, while waterfalls and silent streams and an enormous ice-cold lake succeeded one another throughout the tour. Louise then took me through the Flower Forest and imparted her knowledge about more flowers and plants than I had known to exist. It was almost dark by the time I delivered Louise to her house and returned to the hotel.

I checked out my mountain bike and took a turn around the parking lot to get used to the gears and especially to the saddle which seemed unnecessarily firm. I wheeled it back to the cottage and parked it on the porch.

I had an early dinner all the while trying to recall exactly what had been said between Jean-Pierre and Amaryllis. I knew I should have written it down immediately and now the words were so vague that I could barely recall them. All I knew was that my main impression at the time had been that they were talking about Elizabeth Mattson.

After dinner I changed into my bathing suit.

It was dark—the few minutes between the setting sun and the rising moon—and stepping out on the beach I stood for a moment to become accustomed to the absence of light. The silence was punctuated intermittently by the slapping of the incoming waves and then the swishing sound of their retreat. The palm trees were silhouetted in grotesque forms until with a suddenness that startled me the moon popped up from behind and erased the shadows.

I moved down slowly and walked into the water until it reached my thighs. I plunged in and swam outward, then parallel to the beach, before turning back. I stood in shallow water wringing the salt water out of my hair when I heard faint voices and saw streaks of light flashing across the sand and skirting the tops of trees about a hundred yards away.

I slung the towel around my waist and without further reflection speeded off towards the commotion. Unfortunately I don't always think first and act later—it's rather the other way around. Within a few moments I realized my mistake.

I arrived at the spot where I'd seen the beams of light and joined about ten people watching a pile of wet clothing sloshing about in the water. I stopped abruptly. The lump floated towards us. The waves pushed it up on the sand, then took it back into the water. A stronger wave thrust it almost under my feet and I jumped back. It was not a pair of soaked sweat pants.

It was a bloated body.

A writhing cobra encircled the grotesquely swollen left arm.

CHAPTER 11

'The body of a white man, with a distinctive tattoo of a snake on its left arm, has washed up on the beach near Holetown. Late last night an American private investigator, Jamie Prescott, here on holiday as a travel agent, came upon the gruesome sight when she went out for a seabath around midnight. She was intercepted by the police and spent several hours at the station before being returned to her hotel early in the morning. A police spokesman refused to comment on a possible connection with the two bodies found on the same beach earlier this month. Those two individuals have not yet been identified.'

I pushed the *Barbados Advocate* across the coffee table and thought of Bob Makowski and his bright ideas about peaceful vacation spots. I swear it had taken the flashlight group less than fifteen seconds to disappear from the scene and leave me with the body. A siren bleated, five constables "intercepted" me as I examined the body for signs of life and took me in for questioning. Apparently an anonymous phone call had alerted them.

The front page news item somehow managed to question

why I should have taken a 'seabath' so late at night. Not to mention that the paper had deliberately put me in a false light by implying that I was an investigator posing as a travel agent. And in half an hour I was due for another visit to the police station.

When I arrived I was accosted by two news hounds whom I ignored, and a photographer who managed to snap my picture. A police constable closed the door firmly in their faces but not until I'd heard some rude comments. I had only walked ten steps inside the reception area when the front door opened again and the constable let in a couple of more people.

I recognized them immediately. They were dressed in the same clothes they had on when I saw them at the *Colonial Travel Agency* talking to Louise.

"Oh, is it our Andy?" Mrs. Harris wailed.

"We read about it in the paper," said her husband. "Our Andy 'as a tattoo of a cobra on 'is left arm."

"Oh, but please say it ain't 'im." Mrs. Harris' voice was pitiful and I watched as they were led to an office next to the entrance. The sign on the door said 'Chief Inspector.'

I told the constable at the counter my name. He asked me to wait, said that the Chief Inspector would see me shortly, and would I like some tea? I'd rather have had coffee but settled for tea which was served from a real teapot, was probably made from real tea leaves, and was served in a real cup. The constable carefully poured first the milk, then the tea, and handed me the cup offering me sugar from a bowl. I sat down to wait and to think.

I didn't know why I had been asked back to the station. I had already told the constable on night-duty that I had not known the dead man's name. I had answered all the constable's subsequent questions which had not included whether I had ever seen the man before.

The Harrises were led out a back door presumably to be taken to the morgue for identification of the body. I felt anguish on their behalf because the outcome could not be in much doubt.

I was called in to see the Chief Inspector. He was a tall, elegant, black man in his early 40s, with close-cropped hair. He got up and shook hands politely. Suave. He asked to see my identification and I showed him my PI licence, my travel agent business card, and my passport.

"What were you doing on the beach so late at night?" he asked without preliminaries.

"Just out for a swim." And, although I knew I shouldn't, I added: "Surely that's not a crime."

He stared me down but otherwise didn't react. I decided to hold my acid tongue.

"When I got out of the water I saw a commotion further down the beach. People shouting. People with flashlights."

"The report says you were the only one on the beach. Alone with the body."

I tried to stare *him* down but it didn't work.

"They disappeared when they heard the police siren."

"Did you know the identity of the man?"

"No, Sir."

"Had you seen him before?"

My first sighting of a body flashed before my eyes. I shifted in my chair realizing where the questions were heading.

"Well? Had you seen him before?" The Chief Inspector sounded impatient.

"Yes, I had."

"Where?"

"On my first day here."

"Well?"

"I swam down along the beach and found him floating under water, nearly drowned, by two fishing boats. I swam him back to shore. He was pulled in by a group of guys, he recovered and walked away with them."

"And did you see him again after that?"

Here we go, I thought.

"I did, once."

"And where was that?"

"On the same beach."

"And did you speak to him?" He now looked thoroughly irritated by my curt replies but I had not yet made up my mind whether to drag in Amaryllis.

"No, I never spoke to him," I said. "I don't know his name and he didn't recognize me as the person who had saved his life."

"Could you identify any of his friends?"

The Chief Inspector leaned forward in his chair and looked me straight in the eye. I must have hesitated a moment too long because he looked satisfied he'd caught me. And I must admit I felt no compunction to shield anyone.

"I saw him speak to a woman," I said.

"And did you know who she was?"

"Yes, I did."

"Well?"

"Amaryllis Mattson."

The name hung in the air before dropping with a thud to the bottom of a deep well. I felt quite sure she must be known to the Inspector. As Mel had said, the island was a very small place.

"And where did you observe them speaking?"

"On that same beach."

"And why were you on that beach? I believe your hotel is quite a distance away?"

"I had swum over to take a closer look at the large coral rock."

"And how do you know Miss Mattson?"

I've been a private investigator for almost ten years, I've interrogated scores of people, but I've never been on the witness stand myself. I now felt as if I was, and as good as under oath. Even so, I circumvented the question slightly.

"She is the goddaughter of a Mrs. Louise Higginbotham, the owner of the *Colonial Travel Agency* who is a colleague of mine."

The phone on his desk rang and after an initial 'hello' he listened without speaking. As I watched his face his expression became remote. Then he looked up, found me watching, and avoided my eyes. He ended the call by saying 'fine, fine, fine,' and turned back to me.

"And how long are you planning to stay in Barbados, Miss Prescott?"

Apparently we were not going to talk about Amaryllis. I felt the interview winding down.

"Another week."

"And I assume you will be staying at the same hotel for the duration?"

"Yes, indeed."

The chief inspector got up and extended his hand.

"Thank you for your time, Miss Prescott," he said.

"Not at all," I said sounding very British to my own ears. Accents have a habit of attaching themselves to me.

When I got back to the cottage I found a mountain of a woman on the steps to my porch filling the entire space from rail to rail. She looked at me with protruding frog's eyes, grasped the rail with one hand, pushed off with the other, and hoisted herself upright.

She groaned along with the wooden rail, rearranged her red bandanna and clicked her tongue several times. When she smiled her expression changed into pudgy good nature and everything—eyes, nose, chin—disappeared between her cheeks. She picked up the house-maid's basket with towels, soaps, and other replacements, and stood aside without a word.

"Where's Penelope?" I asked.

"Penelope sick, Madame." She placed a hand approximately where her navel might be, and grimaced to indicate Penelope's affliction. "I am Jeanette."

I detected an accent that didn't sound Bajan.

"Where are you from, Jeanette?"

"From Haiti, Madame. I forget ze kee, Madame."

I let us in and she went directly to the bedroom where she cast a billowing sheet across the mattress. She tucked and stretched and smoothed with her sturdy arms and, at the end, was breathing rather hard. I stayed on the porch while she swept imaginary dust and tidied the kitchenette. She darted quick glances at me as she went and I heard her sing above the rush of water in the bathroom. She moved my three Haitian paintings carefully to straighten the pillows on the sofa but didn't seem to recognize the vivid art from her own country.

I watched her disappear down the garden path, her hips heaving independently of the rest of her body. She had put the basket high on her head and it sat there, improbably, as she swung both arms vigorously, walking fast until she was lost from sight around the bend.

As soon as she was gone I changed into my bikini and headed for the beach. I swam long and hard quite a distance out when, just as I turned back towards land, the surface of the water curled and rippled and out shot three fish, spread their fins and flew by me, elegantly. The one nearest to me, I swear, looked at me and winked. Then they ploughed back into the water and disappeared. I'll never eat any, I promised myself fervently.

When I returned to my chair I was no longer alone. Jean-Pierre was in the one next to mine. He was dressed in working clothes with grubby high-tops. I picked up my towel and dried off while I waited for him to state his case.

"I read about you in the paper," he said curtly.

"Ah, yes."

"Why didn't you tell me you're a private investigator?"

I put on my sunglasses.

"I didn't know I was required to."

Jean-Pierre scratched his beard.

"The guy who drowned, had you seen him before?"

"Why do you ask?" I said.

"No reason. What did the police say? Do they know who it was?"

"Look, I'm sure it'll be all over the papers tomorrow. Why don't you wait and see?"

"I am just curious, *c'est tout.*"

Jean-Pierre leaned back in his chair and we sat in silence.

"By the way," I said at last, "has anyone heard from Elizabeth Mattson?"

"I do not know. I am not a part of the family, I only work there," Jean-Pierre said. His brown eyes had lost their warmth, even his teeth seemed to have lost their shine.

"Oh, I don't know about that," I said. "I thought perhaps you had a feeling for whether her husband and daughter are worried about her. Does she write at all?"

"I know nothing about it," he said and got up. "And you would be well advised to stay out of it."

I looked up at him in surprise.

"What do you mean? Is that some kind of a threat?"

"*Pas du tout,* just some friendly advice." He was moving away.

"You're leaving?" I said.

"Yes. I'll see you around." And he strode off down the beach. I watched him walk away with more energy than I'd seen him display so far. He disappeared at a point beyond the large coral rock where I'd first seen Amaryllis. I sat for a while wondering about the players in this absurd theater.

When I returned to my cottage the lights on the answering machine were blinking furiously. I had messages from Topsy in Bethesda, from Mel Kramer, and from Louise Higginbotham. I returned the call from Louise who picked up on the first ring.

"My dear," she said, "how terribly upsetting for you. I read all about it in the morning paper." She paused. "But I have some disquieting news myself."

"Why, what's happened?"

"Hugh flew to England this morning to be with Elizabeth. She's fallen ill."

"I thought he was out sailing. Did he call you?"

"No, Amaryllis did. And I'm terribly worried," Louise said.

I again regretted that I hadn't jotted down the exact words of the conversation I'd overheard in the library at the plantation between Amaryllis and Jean-Pierre.

CHAPTER 12

The party was a success.

I hadn't realized how far Noelle and Mel's garden stretched down at the back of their house. I stood on the patio and watched close to a hundred people assembled on the lawn under a red awning. A slight wind brought the buzz of their voices in waves towards me. A large buffet was laid out to my left and a tall, ebony waiter filled the plates. Another waiter was on his way down the steps carrying a tray with tall drinks. Three musicians began to beat steel drums in a far corner, and their voices rose in unison, their faces aglitter.

The women were dressed far more elegantly than I, who had packed for scuba-diving and biking. I saw Noelle in a bright red and gold gown speaking to a slim, flat-chested woman in a white mini-skirt—Beth, my dive-master. They stood as the animated center of a group of tall, good looking men, and one enormous woman with a bright hibiscus flower in her hair. I suddenly found myself the focus of their attention. They turned their heads in unison and stared. They are discussing me, I thought. Noelle must have pointed me out, I've become an object of curiosity and—perversely—I raised my glass to them. No one acknowledged my greeting, they just turned away looking guilty so I knew I was right.

"Jamie," exclaimed Mel from behind. "Jamie, the Private Investigator."

Oh, God, I thought, not so loud. I didn't want to spend the rest of the evening explaining myself.

"Shush, you idiot," I whispered.

"Oh, it's too late, people are already talking about you. You'll have to unravel the entire mystery for me later. Here, try the *Mauby*." And he handed me a glass full of a doubtful looking liquid.

"What's this? Another of your famous concoctions?"

"Try it, try it."

"*Mauby?* Sounds hallucinatory."

"You wish. It's simply *Calubrina bark* soaked for hours, strained and chilled. Go on, drink it."

Mel watched me while I took a good swallow.

"It's to die for." I gagged and looked around for something to wash it down with. I found champagne.

"For a detective you show remarkably little curiosity," he said. "Come this way and I'll introduce you around. We've got people from all over. New York, Haiti, Martinique, England. And, Bajans, of course. Take your pick."

I let Mel pick for me and wound up with a group of art dealers from New York. They must have started early—or possibly they had underestimated Mel's concoctions—because they were all glassy eyed. One of them leaned against me and put his head on my shoulder.

"*Lesss* go to your place, honey," he said and slobbered a kiss in the direction of my neck.

"Your wife might object to that," I said, having just been introduced to her.

"No, no, she's already taken care of." He pointed to a tall Bajan who had his arm around her. "So, wassaya say, honey? You got a great ass."

I straightened him up, swung him around, and walked him to a small stone bench which stood against the wall. A few moments later his wife led him away.

I turned to join a different group and found myself looking into the eyes of the Chief Inspector. Neither of us had probably thought we would meet again quite so soon but I shouldn't have been surprised. It seemed that *tout* Barbados had been invited.

"Business or pleasure?" I said.

"Oh, I can assure you, purely pleasure." He looked very elegant and I was wondering what kind of salary a chief inspector pulled down here which allowed him to wear a silk suit and hand-stitched loafers. But maybe he was still single and could splurge it all on his own person.

"And yourself?" he said.

"Oh, myself? The same as you, purely pleasure."

"I hope yesterday's trouble won't prevent you from getting on with your vacation?"

"Oh, no. In fact, tomorrow I take a biking trip across the island to the east coast." I paused. "And have you identified the body yet?"

"Ah, Miss Prescott, but we weren't going to talk business, were we? Let's just say we're still investigating."

And before I could ask about the Harrises the Chief Inspector drifted away smoothly in the fashion of cocktail parties. He joined Noelle's handsome little group and immediately became the center of attention. I went back to the buffet where across the table I saw Jean-Pierre filling his plate with the industry and concentration of the half-starved. He looked up and saw me watching.

He grinned, and his eyes were deep brown again and his teeth Colgate white. He seemed to have forgotten our conversation on the beach. But I hadn't. I automatically looked around for Amaryllis.

"I hear that Hugh Mattson has left for England," I said. "What do you know about his wife's illness?"

He looked at me with a sour expression.
"I know nothing about it."
"And Amaryllis isn't here tonight?"
"I know nothing about her, either."
I laughed.
"That's not what it looked like on the beach the other day."

He didn't have a chance to reply because Noelle came towards us in high heels which sank into the lawn every few steps. Jean-Pierre put down his plate when she reached for his hand.

"Let's dance," she said to him. And to me she said: "You don't mind if I take him away from you?"

I wanted to say, he's not mine to take away, but they were gone. I'd had no idea they were on such familiar terms but can't say I was surprised. The three musicians at the bottom of the garden were drumming in a frenzy and several couples were moving around on a small patch of flagstones. Jean-Pierre was half a head shorter than Noelle. If he'd been taller you'd have said they danced cheek-to-cheek. Noelle was talking and he wasn't answering. Did I detect tension between them. A lover's quarrel?

I looked around for Mel and saw him watching. He had a habit of lowering the hoods over his eyes when he was thinking. They were certainly lowered now.

The music stopped and Noelle returned to me without Jean-Pierre.

"I hope you're enjoying yourself," she said and took my arm. "An incredible crowd, *n'est pas?*"

"Yes, incredible. You have a lot of interesting friends."

"I read about your troubles in the morning paper. You've become quite a celebrity," she said.

"And I don't know why. It's not as if I've accomplished anything to be celebrated for."

"You must understand that in this backwaters anything remotely newsworthy confers celebrity status. Do you have any idea whose body you found?"

"Not a clue," I said. "I don't know anyone here."
"But you're a detective!" Noelle's eyes sparkled. "You can easily find out."
"I'll leave it to the police," I said. "I need to get on with my vacation."
"Ah, *bien sûr,* your biking trip. When are you going?"
"Tomorrow morning bright and early."
"Have fun, *chérie.*"

There was a small commotion at the terrace door. Mel who stood near the buffet turned around and so did I. Then we rushed to the door where Louise Higginbotham stood with tears running down her cheeks.

"Elizabeth is dead. Elizabeth is dead," she wailed. "Amaryllis called to tell me and I rushed over here to find you." She grabbed my arms and held on to me.

We quickly moved her along to the living room and from there outside to my car. We couldn't make out much of what she was saying, all she could do was repeat that Elizabeth was dead.

Half an hour later Mel and I were sitting in Louise's house. We had given her a Valium—produced by Noelle—and Louise had now been sleeping for an hour. Mel and I were waiting for her son, Andrew, to appear.

"Really, you can tell me," Mel said. "Why were you on the beach at midnight?"

"Why? Because I enjoy swimming in the moonlight."

"Alone?"

"But, of course, alone. What are you suggesting? An orgy?"

He quickly stifled a guffaw.

"No. More like the work of a private investigator."

"I can assure you I wasn't looking into anything, I just happened to be in the wrong place at the wrong time."

"I thought you were a travel agent."

"A person can be both." This was getting very tiresome. A distance had been created between us. I'm all too familiar with this phenomenon. People fear I can read their minds—

and discover their past—just by looking at them and they think it safer to stay away from me. And I certainly didn't tell him about my visit with Louise to the plantation.

"It'll be a relief to get out the bike tomorrow and head to the famous east coast," I concluded.

"If you're in the vicinity of Bathsheba around lunchtime you should go to 'Ye Olde Pub,' and get the lobster bisque." Mel looked around listlessly.

Louise's Victorian livingroom was, well, overstuffed. Everything I'd ever seen on a Masterpiece Theater turn-of-the-century series was here.

The wallpaper was actually flocked and pictures in dark frames hung choc-a-block on all available walls. A round table with a fringed tablecloth stood in the middle of the room. Four upholstered chairs had carved mahogany backs. Ceramic pots with ferns stood on several candlestick tables and a collection of porcelain was displayed on a dainty whatnot. A chandelier with opaque glass shades spread murky shadows across our faces.

I studied the many family photographs displayed in elaborate frames on a writing desk recording the life of Louise, her husband, their four sons, and two grandchildren. In one, the beaming boys were lined up leaning on cricket bats, in another, now teenagers, they were clutching surfboards.

"Gordon, Andrew, Albert, and Charles." When Louise had told me their names she had sounded very royal. I also remembered her telling me that Elizabeth Mattson had a horror of being photographed and as I looked around I certainly saw nothing that looked like what I imagined her to be today.

"Oh, there you are, you kind souls." At the sound of Louise's voice Mel and I got up. She looked quite calm and motioned us back to our chairs.

"Amaryllis said that when Hugh got to Hertfordshire where Elizabeth was staying with her relatives, she had been taken to the hospital with pneumonia. She died yesterday before Hugh arrived."

"I am so, so sorry," I said and walked over to Louise. She leaned into my arms briefly and pulled out her handkerchief.

"I hear Andrew at the door," she said. "I'll be quite all right now. You two go back to the party."

"Oh, I don't think so," I said. "I'll be going to the hotel and if you need anything at all, just call me. I'll come see you tomorrow morning."

"But, my dear, you are going biking tomorrow morning. I want you to go on your tour. Andrew will take care of me."

And that's how we left it.

CHAPTER 13

From Holetown I cut east towards Welshman Hall Gully which, according to my guidebook, was a narrow strip of jungle hemmed in by cliffs, and densely covered with plants and trees.

I had called Andrew early in the morning and was told that Louise was still asleep. We agreed again that I should visit her in the evening.

I had filled two bottles with Barbados coral water, dressed in trekking shorts, seamless underwear, a tee, thick socks in Reeboks, and carried a sweatshirt, a cap, wrap-around lightweight sunglasses, and a security belt for my valuables. In the backpack I had my Portable Workshop—which sprouts everything from a bottle opener to a saw—a handful of power bars, and coffee in my thermos.

And off I went.

The bike was running smoothly, mostly uphill, but suddenly the landscape changed and everything went faster. The cropped blanket of the jungle was covered in a fine blue-green mist which blended at the horizon into a purple sheen. But I breezed right through towards the coast since I'd already seen Harrison's Cave and the Flower Forest and wanted to get to Bathsheba before lunch. I passed several rum-shops on the roadside whose proprietors leaned on their staple doors and sent me hopeful glances.

I was in Bathsheba by noon. 'Ye Olde Pub' which Mel had recommended sat high on the cliff overlooking the Atlantic ocean with picture windows towards the narrow strip of beach—its sand coarse brown instead of the inviting white on the west coast. Way below tall waves, stirred up by a brisk wind, were crashing against the rocks sending up a white froth. Obviously, there could be no swimming here.

A transparent fluff of a cloud hung suspended high above the water and, as I watched, its shadows blended into a malicious face with fat cheeks. The face pursed its lips and the mouth curled into a crooked sneer which evaporated as the cloud was stirred up by an invisible stream of air.

The lunch was as good as Mel had promised. Lobster bisque with steamed sweet potatoes, and *cou cou au jus*, the latter being a mash of cornmeal and okra swimming in fish juices. With this I had a perfectly satisfying Chablis and a mixed fruit cup for dessert.

There was no one else in the dining room and the single waiter took his sweet time serving me. It was past one before I could pay my bill and leave.

It was one-thirty by the time I continued down the east coast with Hackleton's Cliff on my right and the rough sea on my left. The road wound up and down, in and out, and slowed my speed to a crawl. The cliff was sometimes close, hanging steeply above the road, sometimes removed as I hugged the road perilously close to an abrupt plunge towards the sea. Several raw patches of ground announced the danger of landslides.

When I was able to pull in at an observation point I was frankly relieved. I leaned the bike against a boulder, sat down on the ground and brought out my thermos. I scrunched down the cap over my ears to prevent my hair from leaving my head in the stiff gale which suddenly blew in from the sea. I sipped coffee.

I continued on the steep road which ran close to the ever more cragged cliff. Less than a mile further south I veered onto a short track which ended at the veritable edge. I didn't get off the bike but straddled it with a foot on either side.

The view was spectacular. To the north was the Scotland district and down below, as far as the eye reached, the rugged limestone coastline. Great gusts of wind made sand and gravel fly violently over the edge and it was several long seconds before I realized something else was wrong.

I turned my head just in time to see a black shadow bear down on me. I glimpsed a pair of huge hands, fingers bent into claws, holding the steering wheel. I had no earthly chance. The car reached me in one unspeakable moment and pushed me towards the precipice.

My hands flew off the handlebar and I went over the edge.

It was all over in a couple of seconds but it felt like hours. I think I must have been screaming because my mouth was wide open. At first I hung on to the bike but it wasn't long before I was separated from it.

I was scared. I was in free fall. My arms flailed in an attempt to grasp at something, anything. I screamed. A storm of stones and earth tumbled down around me into nothing.

Then there was silence.

When I described it later, I liked to say that my life hadn't exactly flashed before my eyes but that I did have a brief vision of myself as Thelma *sens* Louise hurtling through the air over a cliff, hovering for a few interminable moments before dropping towards the abyss. In reality, what had happened was more of a sliding, slamming, and rolling action scraping down the side of the cliff.

I opened my eyes and looked around. My left arm was curled around a thorny bush, my feet were on a ledge. I tried to straighten up and the movement had an immediate effect. Another cascade of stones and earth was released. I pulled to disengage my arm from the bush but thought better of it. It was the only solid grip I could find on anything.

My hands were clammy and the minutes crept by before I dared move again. I let out my breath in a noisy gulp. My ribcage hurt. I moved my feet testing the strength of the ledge by swaying gently back and forth. I turned my head and looked down. I twisted free of the thorny bush, grabbed at a branch which stuck out of the ground and pulled until I was sure it would bear weight. Then I looked around without moving.

The cliff rose steeply with a slight overhang several feet above obscuring the top and preventing me from even guessing how far down I'd fallen.

The side of the cliff was held together by the roots of old bushes and tangled grasses with eroded stones sticking out of its weathered face. Little streams of dry sand and gravel flowed silently and continuously in rivulets towards the bottom as if pushed by an invisible hand.

Without abandoning my saving branch I sat up. My hand was bleeding painfully and I plucked out several sharp thorns from between my fingers and fleetingly thanked the doctors in New York for my recent tetanus shot.

When I looked over the edge I saw my bike hundreds of feet below lying in a crumpled heap.

I looked up. Then down.

My ledge seemed to be somewhere past the middle of the cliff, maybe two thirds down. I saw the deserted beach as a narrow brown line.

The side of the cliff to the left of the ledge tapered downwards in what looked like tiny terraces, two feet wide at the most, with plenty of thorny bushes and sharp grasses sticking out of the sandy wall. Further down I thought I saw several more ledges as wide as the one I was on.

I wiped my bloodied hands on my pants and crawled towards the side of the ledge. I slid down on my stomach, feet first, dug my fingers into the crumbling rock face, found foothold and started the downward journey.

The narrow terraces created by nature were uneven. On the first three or four I succeeded in planting my feet close to the wall and get a good grip. On the fourth I began a painful slide with rocks scraping my face and flaying the skin off my fingers. One of my favorite thorny bushes at last caught my pants in a prickly grip. Then I thudded down onto another ledge.

By the time I reached the bottom I was pretty much beat up. The wind was whipping up the sea and crashed onto the rocks in great gusts. I found the bike almost right away, one wheel missing, the other twisted around itself. My water bottle was gone but I'd hung on to my backpack and the security belt hadn't left my waist.

I made the trek along the beach back to Bathsheba in a little less than an hour. The parking lot at the restaurant was still empty. The waiter observed my disheveled appearance without comment, just showing the whites of his eyes and denying any knowledge of a black car. I went to the restroom, scrubbed my hands and pried out most of the tiny bits of gravel imbedded in the palms. A dose of stinging iodine and some band-aid from the small first-aid kit in my backpack completed the transaction. It felt better but not good.

I persuaded the taciturn waiter to call for a rental car—in the very last minute as it turned out since the garage closed at six—and he, in turn, persuaded them to bring it to me. They came within fifteen minutes.

My return journey from the rugged east coast was slow but uneventful. My ribs ached, my leg muscles were cramping up, blood seeped from my palms and fingertips.

When I reached the hotel the sun had set, stars twinkled between several fast moving clouds and the moon hung low like a silver dollar. Surprisingly, my cottage sat in complete darkness. I stopped to examine the light bulb on the porch and found it missing.

The minute I entered the cottage I knew someone had been through my things. It had been done very carefully and it was probably only because I've tossed a room or two in my investigative career that I noticed the signs. For efficiency

I always pack in see-through zippered plastic bags. And once I arrive I put the bags in drawers but leave them open for easy access.

This evening when I opened the drawers, the bags were zippered up, their contents just slightly rumpled. And my paintings had been moved on their perch on the back of the sofa. I don't, of course, keep any valuables in a hotel room when I'm out. Not even in the safe. Depending on the location, I carry everything on my body tied around my waist.

As far as I could tell nothing was missing,

I stood still and listened. Something knocked against a chair on the porch and I heard stealthy footsteps. I turned out the light and picked up one of my flashlights. My heartbeat rose a notch. I crept along the wall to the doors and slowly pressed the flashlight against the window. I turned on the powerful beam. I saw shadows move and disappear in the distance. Someone now knew I had returned.

I soaked my hands in soap and lukewarm water and bandaged them tightly after picking out a few stray thorns. I'd wait until the morning to decide if I needed medical attention. I would have to report the incident to the Chief Inspector. I wondered if my 'accident' was connected to the drownings. The car had appeared to me as a black shadow. I had no idea of its make. I tried to think who had known about my biking trip and realized that almost everyone did. Jean-Pierre and, through him, Amaryllis. Mel and Noelle and, through them, any number of people at the party. The Chief Inspector. And Louise and her son, Andrew.

I swallowed three Tylenol and went to bed. My sleep was restless and interrupted by several disturbing and confused dreams. I woke up, tossed and turned, drank some water, turned on the light and turned it off, and tossed and turned some more until towards daybreak I slept for an hour. Then it was morning all too soon and the phone rang.

I had totally forgotten my promise to visit Louise.

CHAPTER 14

"Valium," Louise said. "Valium and work. That's what will pull me through. Elizabeth is dead and I feel perfectly devastated."

We were sitting in her office at the *Colonial Travel Agency*. She had just served me a cup of coffee.

"But you mustn't come to rely on a drug," I said, "and you probably shouldn't be driving while you use it." It was obvious that Louise was in a mild state of euphoria.

"Andrew dropped me off and he's coming back for me in the evening."

"Er, and what have you heard from the plantation?" I said.

Her hand shook when she put down her coffee cup.

"Andrew talked to Amaryllis—they went to school together, you know—she says Hugh is returning in a few days." Louise started shaking. "He is burying Elizabeth in England. And I don't even know where. She would have wanted to come back home."

She shuddered violently and I went over to put my arm around her. She made a valiant effort to compose herself and poured more coffee. When I stretched out my hand for the cup she looked at the band-aids in my palms and almost dropped the coffee pot.

"My dear Jamie, whatever happened to your hands?"

I told her about my free-fall down the side of the cliff.

"But who would want to hurt you?" she said. Her face was white and her teeth jutted out aggressively. "It must have been a mistake."

I thought of dead bodies. I thought of the entire incestuous group of islanders—both native and expatriate—none of whom I felt entirely comfortable with. I thought of the mountain bike at the bottom of the cliff, of the tennis games I never got to play and wouldn't now because of my ripped palms. I thought of the scuba diving I wouldn't continue for the same reason. I couldn't take the chance of fresh blood sending a message to sharks.

"No," I said. "No, I don't think it was a mistake."

"Owww," someone said from the door. "'ow are you, Miss 'igginbotham?" and in walked the Harrises looking like boiled lobsters.

"My, my, my," Louise fussed and got up from behind her desk. "You really shouldn't be out without a sun cream. Do you have good news about your son?"

Their faces fell and I realized I hadn't told Louise about the identity of the body I had found washed up on the beach.

"Louise." I stood up and took her aside. "Mr. and Mrs. Harris thought they recognized the description of Andy's tattoo in the newspapers. I saw them at the police station. They were taken to the morgue to identify the body."

"Oh, my dears, I am so sorry." Louise had tears in her eyes.

"It wasn't Andy." Mrs. Harris sat down abruptly on the chair I'd just vacated.

"*What?*" My voice reverberated against the far wall. "*What?*"

"You see, Miss, our Andy 'as a tattoo of another kinda snake, this one wasn't our Andy's."

"But, then, where *is* Andy?" I could have bit my tongue

because this question set off a wail from Mrs. Harris and loud moans from Mr. Harris.

"We 'ave walked up and down the beach and we 'ave asked 'undreds of 'orrible people. But they pretend they don't know 'im."

"And the police," Louise said. "Can't the police help you search? What do they tell you? Surely they must consider him a missing person now?"

The Harrises looked at one another briefly and lowered their eyes.

"Ow," he said at last. "We're not important people. They say to just wait, that 'e'll show up sooner or later."

"Well, I never," Louise said in her most indignant voice. "Now, you just let me handle this. I'll soon set them straight."

She went to the back and we could hear her voice rise and fall, pause, fall and rise, until she put down the phone sharply and returned to us with a satisfied smile.

"There," she said. "I spoke directly to Bundy, the Chief Inspector. He went to school with my oldest son, Gordon, you know. He'll start looking for Andy. And I told him to take good care of you, too, my dear," she said to me. "Don't deal with anyone minor, go directly to him."

The claustrophobic relationships continue, I thought. Amaryllis and Andrew and Gordon and Bundy—the Chief Inspector, whose name made him sound less a chief inspector than a rambunctious school boy—and who knew who else.

The Harrises left and soon after I did, too. On my way, reluctantly, to the police station to report my 'accident'.

Bundy was in his office looking official despite Louise's exhortations and didn't get up when I was shown in. He looked at me with an expression of 'what, that bloody woman again,' and pointed distractedly to a hard chair. By now I knew I wasn't really there to report my accident but to find out more about Andy. I started out by recounting my over-the-cliff experience mainly to obtain a police report for my insurance company.

Bundy scribbled conscientiously on a white police form and duly noted my bandaged hands. I now realized I should seek medical attention to add another form to my insurance file. I made a mental note to ask Louise for a referral.

"I have just come from visiting with Louise Higginbotham," I said. "How very sad about her friend Elizabeth Mattson dying in England. I'm sure you must have called Amaryllis with condolences. How is she taking all this?"

Bundy glared at me and I could see conflicting thoughts roll across his forehead. I had no idea why he felt I shouldn't assume that he knew Amaryllis. Maybe it was just that 'beware-of-private-investigator' syndrome.

"She is obviously devastated," Bundy admitted. "And so are we all."

"I imagine she is also upset that her friend, Andy, seems to have disappeared. I ran into the Harrises just now and they told me the body I found was not Andy's."

"I trust you are not investigating?" His tone was abrupt.

"Certainly not," I said just as abruptly and at that very moment decided to investigate. "I'm going to leave it to you, of course. It's just that everyone is saying that three dead bodies on the beach seems to be somewhat excessive."

I asked for a copy of the police report about my accident, waved my hand to Bundy across his desk rather than submitting it to another Bajan handshake and departed. Five minutes later I was on my way to the Granger-Farley plantation.

As usual, clouds of dust rose on the unpaved road and I slowed down as I drove through the sugarcane fields. I passed the sugar mill and a few minutes later, partly hidden by swaying banana plants, saw the plantation manager's small house. Jean-Pierre's jeep was nowhere in sight.

I cruised down the tree-lined entranceway where the velvety beige sheep with their black bellies lifted their heads briefly to appraise me with olive eyes. When I arrived at the tall wall surrounding the plantation house I was surprised to see that an iron gate—as tall as the wall—was now in place. I coasted to a stop, parked under a couple of shady palm trees, and looked around. No cars were parked outside.

When I was here before the iron doors had nestled against the inside of the wall. There were now deep scrape marks on the ground where the bottom of the doors had been dragged across to a closed position. I flipped the handle on the old-fashioned square locking mechanism. It clicked sharply and the gate swung open a couple of inches before a rasping noise made me look down at a heavy chain slung across the bottom rungs. It effectively held the doors together and blocked the entrance.

A narrow footpath almost obscured by weeds ran along the outside of the wall and, bending down under the overhanging trees, I decided to follow it to the left of the gate. Small piles of debris were heaped on the path at frequent intervals looking as if a gardener had pushed them there, out of the way, in a lazy effort to avoid removing them in a wheelbarrow. The path slowly widened and veered away from the side of the wall. The surrounding bushes looked better tended and the grass was cut around a freshly dug trench which ran on about ten feet. After pushing my way through a tangle of bushes I suddenly emerged in front of the small chapel.

I took a step forward in surprise and then, just as quickly, stepped back in case anyone was looking. After finding the front gate locked I had a distinct feeling someone didn't want company.

I was now standing far enough from the wall to see the top story of the plantation house and even, on tiptoe, the library windows on the ground floor. I had stood there with Hugh Mattson when he pointed in the direction of the chapel and it had been obscured by trees with only the red roof visible. I figured that if anyone happened to be looking out those same windows right now they couldn't see me.

I walked forward slowly, damning my yellow t-shirt which made me a beacon of light. The vestry door was open and I went inside. The room slowly came into focus. First the stone bench built into the wall under the window. Then the narrow trestle table. And then the massive door leading into the chapel itself. The air hummed with quiet and shadows moved across the walls in reflection of swaying palm trees outside the vestry window.

My eyes were now perfectly adjusted to the semi-darkness. Elizabeth's prayer book sat on the trestle table with her handkerchief on top. Her pink cardigan which had hung on a wooden peg on the wall now lay neatly folded on the stone bench. The garden tools had disappeared and the wooden clogs were covered in fresh mud. Footprints returning from the front door were clearly visible on the dusty floor.

Stepping back towards the door I followed the footprints outside to the stoop. There they disappeared. The door screeched loudly when I closed it. Then I walked around the east side of the chapel and continued until I reached the two ancient tombs. A rusty wheelbarrow lay overturned on its side a few feet to the left.

I walked in between the lichen-covered slabs and rested a hand lightly on each. The one on my left sat intact as I remembered it and the one on my right had the same cracks going across. In fact, I now noticed that the cracks went right through the slab and separated it into several pieces. I placed both hands at the edge of the smallest piece, braced my feet against the other tomb, and pushed as hard as I could. A few pebbles fell to the ground and slowly the slab began to move.

It was when I stopped to get a better grip on the stone and had just bent down to push it to the edge to get a look inside the tomb, that I was struck a sharp blow on the back.

CHAPTER 15

I let go of the slab, pitched sideways with my hands on the ground and my face in the gravel. In the three seconds it took me to get my bearings I was struck again, this time by a kick from behind. The blow glanced off my thigh but propelled me further into the ground.

I was now on all fours scrambling to get up. When I turned around I looked straight into Amaryllis's contorted face.

"You bloody woman," she screamed.

"Whoa, there!" I sought for a better foothold on the ground and found it.

"You bloody snoop." She came towards me with raised hands, her fingernails pointing towards my face.

When she was close enough I swiftly grabbed her by the wrists and held her away to avoid her kicking feet. We stood like that until she suddenly went limp. I let go of her and stepped back to a safer distance.

"I'm sorry," I said. "I'm sure you were startled to see me. I'm looking for Andy."

"Andy?" She stared at me with cold eyes and tight lips. "How do you know Andy?"

"Oh, I get around."

"Yes, I've heard about your snooping. Why would you look for him here?"

"Well, *you* tell *me*."

"Bitch!"

In a flash, she bent down behind the wheelbarrow and came back up gripping a small trowel.

I barely had time to get into a *tae kwon do* stance for a forward kick—straightening my back, relaxing my shoulders, and tensing my abdomen—before she hurtled towards me, the sharp edge of the trowel aimed at my face.

I was ready. When she was three feet away my right foot was in the air, my arms flailed, air left my lungs in a mighty rush, I made contact, and the trowel sailed out of her hand and landed some fifteen feet away.

Amaryllis sat down hard on the ground and pressed her right hand into her side.

"You're trespassing," she shouted. "I'll call the police."

"Maybe *I* should do that. I've just been attacked with a deadly weapon."

"It was self defense. You were trespassing."

"Why don't we call it even." I stepped back and around the tomb. Then I casually leaned on the slab, pushed it over the edge and stared into the dark interior.

"What are you bloody doing? Put that slab back."

"Sorry, too heavy," I said. "I'm leaving."

Turning my back—and feeling slightly vulnerable—I walked quickly towards the house and my car.

The tomb had been empty.

I drove back to the hotel looking in the rearview mirror for signs of Amaryllis in her little red MG but the road was nearly empty.

When I got back to the cottage I found Mel and Noelle waiting on my doorstep.

"We were in the neighborhood and thought we'd take you out to an early dinner," Noelle said and stretched out her rather heavy legs.

Mel offered me his hand but let it hang in the air when I didn't grasp it. In explanation I held out my palms and he looked at the bandages in stupefaction.

"Yes," I said. "I had an accident on your rugged east coast. I was pushed over the edge of the cliff deliberately."

After I'd told them in detail what had happened Noelle exclaimed:

"*Mon Dieu*, why would anyone do this to you?"

"I can only surmise it has something to do with the newspaper account describing me as a private investigator," I said. "If someone's trying to scare me off the island they're succeeding. I've just about had it."

I went inside to change and then we sat on the porch with rum punches and watched the sun set. The sky turned a fiery crimson and purple, a cool breeze stirred the dry fronds of the palm trees, fireflies glowed in the abrupt darkness and crickets and frogs suddenly became voluble.

"We actually came by earlier to watch you play tennis," Mel said and his voice sounded muted in the increasing darkness. "I bet you play a damn good game. I've wanted to take it up again but I've got this bum knee."

"Nonsense," Noelle said. "You've wanted nothing of the kind and you don't have a bum knee. You've just become plain lazy. The island's gotten to you."

Mel put down his glass rather sharply. "We're taking you to a restaurant on the beach, they have dancing and a limbo show," he said to me.

"Very Caribbean." I sighed. "Just what I need."

The music, with some bravura drumming, could be heard into the street. The building sat right on the ocean, the decor was vaguely nautical, the candle-lit tables covered with white tablecloths. After we were seated I successfully avoided a discussion about my friends, the flying fish. Instead, I considered such appetizers as spiced pumpkin and lentil soup, or sauteed shrimp, and a choice of entrées of grilled barracuda with cou-cou, or pepperpot stew, or baked snapper in coriander sauce.

The atmosphere suddenly became electric. Drumbeats rolled across the room and smothered our voices. The lights dimmed except for a single spotlight on the dance floor, now empty. A pole, held by two women dressed in bikinis and grass skirts, was placed crosswise a few feet from the floor. A glistening black male dressed only in white pants rolled up to the knees, came onto the platform in a flying leap.

The drums sounded hushed in the sudden quiet until the slow pulsations changed into a rapid crescendo which seemed to lift the man off his feet. He bent backwards, held out his arms and slipped under the pole. Then he jumped high in the air and acknowledged the enthusiastic applause from the room. The pole was lowered to a few impossible inches above the floor, the drums sounded and the man repeated his feat.

The drumming was replaced by electric guitar and the floor filled up with tourists trying to emulate the smooth steps of the Bajan couples. Noelle pulled up Mel and they danced away across the floor.

I took this moment to retire to the restroom at the back. It was jam-packed with women combing and spraying their hair, repairing their make-up, chatting away. When I stood at the sink to wash my hands and glanced into the mirror the image I saw was not mine but that of Amaryllis.

She stared back at me.

"Oh, it's *you!*" she said. Disdain was in her eyes and in her voice. Her spiked hair stood up aggressively. She wore a bit more than on the beach, but not much. A transparent blouse through which everything could be seen. A micro skirt up which much was revealed. Long bare legs and slim feet in sandals.

I said nothing, finished drying my hands and returned to the restaurant, pushing my way between chairs and tables and people getting up to dance. Mel and Noelle were back at the table and we dawdled over soursop ice-cream and coffee.

When the dance music resumed Mel took his turn with me. He steered me to the edge of the floor, held me away at arm's length to look at me, laughed, pulled me close and placed his cheek firmly against mine, dancing slowly against rhythm.

"We're compatible," he murmured in my ear and if I could have moved my head I would have concurred. He was a couple of inches taller than I and that, to a tall woman, is always a blessing. But he steered me with an iron hand and that soon made me want to squirm out of his grip.

The dance floor was full and I caught a fleeting glimpse of Amaryllis snug in the arms of a tall black Bajan and then—to my surprise—Jean-Pierre François dancing with Noelle. Mel must have noticed them as soon as I did because his grasp around my waist slackened and his cheek left mine. He slid us forward smoothly, swirled into their wake, let go of me, grabbed Noelle and thrust me into the arms of Jean-Pierre.

"Time to switch partners," Mel yelled. Noelle at first looked annoyed but recovered quickly and put both arms around Mel's neck. They bounced away.

Jean-Pierre's cheek reached me approximately to my chin, he held me loosely and felt disturbingly familiar when he brushed his beard softly against me. Pavlov again, I smiled to myself. I looked down into his warm brown eyes.

"And why isn't a good-looking guy like you married?" I said.

"*Pardón?*"

"Or have you left a little wife behind in Quebec?"

"*Mon Dieu.* Why do you say that? To be sure, you must be joking."

"Of course. I don't know what got into me."

He looked at me suspiciously. Then he pulled me closer.

"She'll get me in trouble," he whispered and glanced around for Amaryllis. "I want to leave the job but I have a contract."

I laughed.

"Contracts can be broken. What're they gonna do, tie you to a tree?"

"She'll cause trouble. Accuse me of something."

"She could. Sexual harassment is everywhere."

"No, not that kind of trouble. Mon Dieu," he groaned, "nothing like this has ever happened to me before."

"*Mon Dieu* is right. It seems she has you by the short hairs."

He let me go abruptly. We had stopped in front of my table where Mel and Noelle now sat glaring at one another either at the beginning or at the end of an argument. Amaryllis was perched on my chair.

"I'll have another coffee," I said. "And I'd like my chair, please."

"*I'd like my chair, please,*" she mimicked. But she got up, walked around to Jean-Pierre and pressed her body into his so fast and hard that his arms went around her automatically. She dragged him away with a saucy grin first at me, then at Noelle.

When we left fifteen minutes later I could feel her eyes at my back when we passed their table on our way out. I had a fleeting glimpse of two hefty men dressed in black, and two more women dressed as scantily as Amaryllis.

Mel and Noelle—on the verge of a fight—drove me back to the hotel and we parted without ceremony. When I got to my cottage I noticed that the electric bulb above the front door had been replaced. It gave out a sharp, bright glare. I went inside and retrieved two phone messages, one from Topsy asking me to call. And one from Louise asking me to lunch the next day.

I got ready for bed before stepping out on the porch. I sat there breathing deeply, listening to the noises of the night. I looked at the silhouette of a group of palm trees at the edge of the garden, their leaves fluttering silently in the wind. I stood up to lean on the rail, peered at the twisted undergrowth and listened to the crickets serenading each other.

Then I gasped in surprise. A tall man stood motionless, glued to the front of a tree trunk as if he had stopped short to weather some danger. His dark clothes blended perfectly with the tree. It was the slight movement of his head and a flash of white which had made me aware of him.

The movement stopped but the minute I took a step back the man raised his arms and moved swiftly across the grass towards the deck. I automatically got into a jumping kick stance, raised my left foot, ready to spring into the air. As it turned out, he stopped before he got to the steps. Instead of advancing he put both hands on the railing and raised his face to mine. I abandoned *tae kwon do* and stared. It was Tattoo.

"I'm Andy, Andy Harris," he whispered.

His face disappeared and instead he came crawling up the steps to the porch.

"Shhhh," he whispered. "They can 'ear you."

"Who? Who can hear me?"

"Shhhh. Please let me in. *Please.*" He scuttled towards the door, pushed it open and flung himself inside on the floor.

"Don't put on the light. *Please.* It's all too 'orrible."

I eventually had him settled in a chair in the darkness and got the story out of him.

It seemed that he had arrived in Barbados two months ago on his very first trip abroad intending to stay two weeks. He had rented a cheap room close to the beach and had met Amaryllis on the first day. He had never encountered anyone like her.

"I became 'er bloody slave," he said with a shudder. "She's a bloody vulture."

In short order he graduated from his occasional use of pot to cocaine, canceled his return reservations, ran out of money, gave up his cheap room, and slept on the beach.

"She let me shower and sleep at 'er father's house when 'e was away."

"Is she dealing drugs?"

"I got mine from 'er."

"Who dumped you from the boat?" I asked.

"Big black guy. Don't know 'is name, do I? Goes around with 'er. I told 'im I wouldn't deal. 'E said 'e'd bloody well finish me off. Nearly did." He sniffled. "The chaps told me you brought me in. Ta. Read about the body—the one with a tattoo like mine—washing up on the beach."

"Did you know him?"

"Bloke from New Zealand. Called 'imself Prince, didn't 'e? No good to 'im now. I been 'iding out since they found 'im."

"Do you know where they get the drugs?"

"Ow, 'course not, they wouldn't of told me, now would they?" He looked away furtively.

"But surely you must suspect someone? Who were the two guys who chased you on the beach?"

Andy shook his head, slumped down in the chair, closed his eyes, and said 'ow' a few more times. I decided it was no use and my trusted inner voice told me to stay away from whatever it was I had now stumbled upon.

"Your parents are here looking for you," I said instead and, startled, he opened his eyes and stared at me.

"Ow, no way. They don't 'ave money for a trip to Barbados. What a bloody mess. They shouldn't get involved. They gotta leave."

"You will all have to leave, Andy. You'll stay here for what's left of the night. In the morning I'll see to it that you all get a flight out of here immediately."

Needless to say, Andy slept like a baby while I sat up for a couple of hours staring out the window at the gradual dawn. In the morning I ordered an extra breakfast tray and waited until I could call Louise at the agency.

CHAPTER 16

The death notice—asking people to refrain from condolence visits—was in both daily morning newspapers.

The *Barbados Advocate* carried a short obituary mentioning Elizabeth Mattson's charitable works and detailing her illustrious family background going back to the 1790s. The Grantleys and the Farleys had eventually joined their sugar plantations through prudent marriages, survived the slave rebellions in the early 1800s, and had been compensated by the British government for their loss of slave labor caused by the abolition of same in 1834. By the 1880s and through the 1900s the family married into the newly created merchant class which provided the money for continuing the sugar plantation. There was mention at the end of Hugh Mattson's current efforts to diversify the crop. All in all, an influential and respected family in Barbados society.

I read the paper while Louise was on the phone with the airlines using her considerable persuasive skills—and a familiarity with the agent who most likely had gone to school with one of her four sons—to secure three seats for the

Harrises on a supposedly fully booked flight to London that same afternoon.

"You'd better go get Andy," she said briskly when she hung up the phone. "And I'll go to Prospect Bay and collect his parents. We'll meet back here in an hour. Then I will personally take them to the airport and make sure they leave without further trouble."

When I arrived at the hotel Andy was huddled in a corner of the room, his hair stringy and wet, his face bloodless and his gums, when he attempted a smile at me, fiery red. Judging from the unmistakable aroma which wafted towards me as soon as I opened the door, the butt he tried to hide in his half-closed fist was pot.

"All right," I said and opened the door to the porch to create a through draft. "You'll have to give it up, you're about to embark on your home journey and we can't send you off carrying a fistful of reefers and have you arrested before you even get on the plane."

"Don't 'ave any more, this was the last," he said miserably and almost swallowed the glowing tip before he let it go with an expletive.

"Oh, go clean your teeth," I said and gave him an unused brush and a tube of paste. "You can keep it." It'll be his only luggage, I thought.

Half an hour later we walked into the *Colonial Travel Agency* where Andy had a tearful reunion with his parents. The tears were mostly his mother's. His father embraced him awkwardly and patted his back, and the three of them then sat down and stared past one another in embarrassed silence. So much for parental communication.

Louise got busy re-issuing their tickets and answering several phone calls. After a few minutes she got up briskly— her cheeks had assumed some hectic patches and her nose looked more prominent than usual—handed the Harrises their tickets and instructed them to wait until she pulled up her car in front of the agency. Within ten minutes she was there and I waved them off.

Topsy had left another message on my machine at the cottage this time sounding exasperated because I hadn't returned her first call and saying 'Jamie, I really need to talk to you'. I picked up the phone and got her at the office on the second ring.

"Topsy," I exclaimed. "I am so sorry I didn't return your call at once."

"Never mind, I'm just glad you're having a good time."

"No, no, I'm not really, it's not that, I've run into a couple of issues . . . ."

"Issues? What issues? Have you gotten involved in something?"

"Not really. I've been busy having a good time." It sounded lame and, face-to-face, Topsy wouldn't have believed me but, somehow, static and distance made her ignore my vacillations.

"I hate to bring you bad news but I need you to come home." Topsy seemed uncharacteristically down.

I listened to her list of bad news. Margo, our hitherto totally dependable travel agent had quit suddenly without giving notice. Julie, Topsy and Jack's twenty-year old daughter, had injured her back on a skiing trip to Colorado and was in a hospital near her campus at UCLA. Topsy and Jack were leaving for the airport as she spoke. The affairs of Prescott Travel, Inc. were in the uncertain hands of Kristy, the gofer who doesn't do coffee.

"But there's good news, too." Topsy always regains her sunny equilibrium faster than I do. "Today is only Friday. I've put up a sign that we're closed tomorrow so, strictly speaking, you don't have to leave Barbados until Sunday." There was a pause and, then: "Can you manage, Jamie?"

"Of course, I can." I gave my voice an upward lilt. "I'll be home by Monday. Give my love to Julie and kick Margo for me if you can find her. And don't worry about my vacation.

I've just about had it, anyway." And ain't that the truth, I thought, feeling a certain relief that matters had been taken out of my hands.

When we hung up I started out by packing my suitcase and placing my paintings in the cardboard box Noelle had provided for them. I went to the lobby and informed the registration clerk I would be leaving Sunday morning and to cancel the tennis I'd not yet managed to play. I decided to stop by in person to cancel the dives with Beth.

The realization that I would soon leave suddenly infused the island with glamour and romance. The sand looked whiter, the water a warmer blue, the sky brighter, the people more colorful, the roads perfectly navigable. I steered the car along the left side without a second thought, up the so-called platinum coast, passing sumptuous golf courses, gorgeous private homes and swank hotels.

By the time I reached the parking lot above Beth's diveshop I felt properly nostalgic for a place I had known only ten days. But even as I thought, oh, I'll be back, I knew myself well enough to realize I probably wouldn't. I don't enjoy back-tracking, my *modus vivendi* is forward motion.

When I got to the wooden stairs leading from the parking lot to the beach I stopped and watched. One of Beth's speedboats had been pulled up on the sand and two men were carrying scuba gear ashore and into the hut which served as her office. Third dive, I thought, which meant that Beth would probably be through for the day. I could invite her to dinner.

I continued down the steps just as one of the men returned the boat to the water and roared away down the coast. When I got closer to the hut I heard raised voices and hesitated outside the door. There was no reason for me to eavesdrop, just one of the bad habits I can't seem to shake.

"In plain daylight," Beth was saying. "What's got into you. Don't you ever dare do that again, he would kill you."

And, then, in the unmistakable voice of Jean-Pierre François: "*Mon Dieu mà chérie,* I missed you, and no one saw me."

I knocked on the door and stepped inside before anyone could tell me not to. They pulled apart as if a fuse had been lit under them.

"Sorry." I smiled. "Didn't mean to interrupt."

Beth recovered nicely.

"Nothing to interrupt." She, too, smiled.

Jean-Pierre—whose mobile face had more difficulty looking inscrutable—floundered about in the limited space and headed towards the door.

"Oh," I said. "Please don't leave on my account. I didn't realize you go in for scuba diving, as well?"

"No, yes, *bién,* I've been thinking of taking some lessons."

"But now that he's learned that certification will take some effort, he's decided against it," Beth said.

"Yes, *evidement,* I seem to be more suited to land than to water. Well, nice to meet you but I must be going."

He escaped.

"I took him down once." Beth said. "He's not the diver type, got claustrophobia. And what can I do for you? You're not scheduled for today."

I didn't answer but just stared at the floor. Was that the cask I'd seen under water wedged into the coral reef and wrapped in seaweed? I stepped across the diving gear piled next to it. It was a metal box and it hadn't come from an ancient ship-wreck. Stripped of the seaweed it looked brand new. I retreated from the water which had collected in a small pool on the floor.

"I see that you recognize the box from the reef," Beth said. She took a hold of the metal handles and hefted the box to the table.

She opened the box with a flourish and I peered inside. It was completely dry. And empty.

"It's very well sealed," I said. "Not a drop of water. How mysterious. I wonder where it came from."

"It's been sitting here on the floor since yesterday," she said. "One of the guys finally brought it up because I was curious. And to answer your question, I don't know where it came from, there are no markings. But it looks rather useful and I've decided to use it for tools. Now, what can I do for you?"

I observed her sallow skin and the black roots in her bleached hair and felt I hadn't really looked at her before. Her dark eyes obscured her thoughts and her thin lips concealed her teeth even when she smiled. I realized I'd never heard her laugh. She was no taller than Amaryllis and looked a few years older but her flat chest and thin body didn't give out the same sexy vibrations. If I had interpreted her remarks correctly, she had a jealous boyfriend. So what was Jean-Pierre doing here? Probably just fishing in every pond. Like Roger, I thought. A busy man. Amaryllis, Noelle, Beth. And me, if I'd let him.

"I'll be away for a couple of days," I said. "I'll let you know when I can resume our dives. Just thought I'd come by in person to tell you."

"I appreciate that." Beth closed the lid on the box and put it back on the floor. "I'll be seeing you then next week?"

"Sure," I said not at all sure why I hadn't told her I was about to leave the island for good. And forget about the dinner invitation.

When I arrived back at the hotel I found Louise's son, Andrew, waiting for me.

CHAPTER 17

The first words he said to me were:
"She's all right."
"What has happened?"
"There's been an accident."
"But Louise is all right? Where did it happen? Was she alone?"
"No, she was not alone."
"Andy? His parents?"
Andrew put his hand on my arm and led me away from the parking lot towards my cottage.
"Someone ran them off the road into a gully. Good thing they weren't going that fast. My mother was bruised by the seatbelt and they took her to the hospital as a precaution. The Harrises just had some minor scratches. It's Andy. Andy has disappeared."
"Disappeared?"
"My mother says two men came running down the cliff and took him. It happened on that stretch of deserted road where it veers towards the coast."
I thought of the car that had pushed me over the top of a different cliff and suddenly felt on the verge of throwing

up. I could see it now—the headline in next week's *Barbados Advocate*: 'Unidentified body washes up on beach at daybreak.'

"No, don't take me to the cottage," I said. "I would like to see your mother."

"My brothers are with her but I will certainly take you to see her if it will make you feel better. She's rather shaken but really, she's remarkably fine."

When we got there the first people we met were Mel and Noelle.

"We've just come from there," Mel said. "She's sleeping and the doctor wants her to rest until the morning. They're not allowing any more visitors."

Andrew went in to be with his brothers and Noelle said: "We'll give you a ride back to your hotel."

"No, we'll do better than that," said Mel. "We'll all go out to dinner. We have to eat, don't we?"

We stopped at the cottage so I could change. I looked around in some surprise having expected to find the bed made and the kitchenette and bathroom cleaned up. I called housekeeping.

"Yes, Madam?"

"This is Jamie Prescott in cottage 3-H. Just wanted to let you know that Jeanette hasn't been by yet to clean up."

"Jeanette, Madam?"

"Yes, the maid."

"Madam, we have no maid called Jeanette."

"Then who has been cleaning my cottage?"

"Penelope, Madam."

"I thought you sent a substitute because Penelope was sick?"

"Not as far as I can see from the chart, Madam."

"Well, no matter, would you just be good enough to send someone around?"

"Right, Madam."

Even the best hotels screw up, I reflected, and got into my cerise sun dress which went well with my deepening tan. My hair looked a little the worse for exposure to sun and salt water and neither shampoo nor conditioner had helped much. I grabbed my backpack. Not the most fancy eveningwear accessory but I gotta work with what I have.

No one from housekeeping had shown up by the time I joined Mel and Noelle but owing to my new-found island mentality I didn't call them back. By seven we were on our way down the coast to a seaside restaurant. It turned out to be local in flavor, small and secluded, without a touristy floor show. We sat on the small terrace at a round table, our chairs facing the ocean. A full moon hung low, its icy shadows hidden by the fiery reflection of a reluctant sun. Brilliant insects buzzed against a lantern in the deepening dusk. A string of flat-cropped acacias framed tiers of luminous sand, dark blue water, and a shimmering horizon. The shadow of a fishing boat rose and dipped on faint ripples moving towards shore.

We ate seafood with spicy sauces and our wine glasses seemed to fill up by themselves. Noelle was wearing a gold bracelet with tiny rubies which flashed in the candlelight.

I leaned back in my chair and listened to the sounds of crickets and the metallic clicks of insects on the corrugated roof above the terrace. The white moon was now in full control of the night sky where stars blinked on and off in a constantly wavering circuit.

"Who could have run Louise off the road," I said.

"Bundy has taken charge, the police will investigate," Noelle said. "I wouldn't worry about it if I were you."

"You mean I should keep my nose out of it?" I immediately regretted my tone of voice. "Oh, so sorry, didn't mean to be obnoxious. It's just that this reminds me of my own so-called accident getting rammed from behind."

"I'm sure Bundy will figure it all out." Noelle beckoned to the waiter and asked for the dessert menu.

"Hugh Mattson seems to be recovering well from the death of his wife," I said. "I saw him load up his boat and go sailing with a bunch of friends."

I looked at Noelle waiting for a reaction. Nothing. I looked at Mel. Nothing. I don't care, I thought. Let them sort out their own problems.

"What are we having?" Noelle said. "Do we all want coffee? I'm having the fruit salad. You, too, Mel? And Jamie, how about you?"

"Okay, I'll go with the fruit salad." I felt a need for something soothing after the *conkies* Mel had recommended and which upon my prudent inquiry had turned out to consist of pumpkin, sweet potatoes, cornmeal, coconut, and some unidentifiable spices, steamed in banana leaves. Tasty but fiery.

When Mel excused himself and left the table for a few minutes, I turned to Noelle.

"Enjoy your sail with Hugh?" I said.

"*Oh, la, la,* you saw me? Sure I enjoyed it. Nothing exciting ever happens here and he keeps fun company." Her voice was casual. "Just don't tell Mel."

I won't, I thought, but someone else is sure to.

We were the last guests to leave, walking slowly to the car. We drove in silence and I sat with my head against the back of the front seat which Noelle had insisted I take, eyes closed. I opened them only when I felt the car turn sharply and speed up the road towards the hotel. The stars had dimmed and dark clouds hovered just above the palm trees. When we came further up the road the light on the horizon grew brighter as if an early dawn was just beyond the trees. The clouds now raced full speed across the sky.

I stared and sniffed at the air which wafted in sudden gusts through the open windows of the car.

"Is that smoke?" I exclaimed.

Gravel shot out behind the back wheels as Mel accelerated and screeched into the driveway to the parking lot. I leaned on the dashboard and strained to see through the murky undergrowth. When I looked up higher I saw tall tree trunks sway and flicker in the hot air which vibrated against the orange sky.

We were out of the car in a flash, running down the path towards the beach, suddenly surrounded by a crowd of people from the hotel. Someone shouted for everyone to stay back, but I pushed my way through followed by Mel and Noelle. When we reached the last bend in the path the intolerable heat forced us to stop.

I dug my nails into Mel's arm and gasped.

My cottage was lit from within with contained heat. The windows glowed amber, yellow, and orange, until the glass burst one after the other in sharp explosions. The flames leapt into the night, knifing the darkness with hissing sounds, licking their way around the porch, around the door frame, and down the stair railing. The roaring fire was fed by the dry night air and towering flames shot straight up.

I moved closer. I held my arms tightly around my waist and flinched when flames exploded above the porch and brought the roof crashing down in front of the staircase. At the sound of splintered wood and shattered glass I pulled back. I then got shoved aside when fire-fighters dragged a hefty hose through the underbrush and ordered everyone out of the way.

Mel and Noelle insisted on staying with me and we went to the hotel terrace where Mel ordered three stiff drinks. That was when Bundy, the Chief Inspector, joined us. He refused a drink and contrived to look very official. He pulled out a notebook and poised his pen above it.

"Miss Prescott," he said in a soft voice—and I couldn't determine if it was soft in deference to my recent shock or exasperated because of our continuing confrontations. "Miss Prescott, you have an unexplained way of getting in harms way. I must ask you to make a full statement about the real reason you are in Barbados and if you are in any way investigating privately into criminal activities you must disclose the facts so that we can take the necessary measures to protect you. I would suggest that the best you can do is to cease your snooping and return to your own country immediately."

"I assure you, Inspector, I came here on an entirely private vacation," I began. "Your constables found me near the body on the beach by accident and I disclosed everything I knew. I still don't know who it was and, I might add, I am wondering why you are keeping it under wraps. I reported my accident on the east coast to you immediately and I haven't been informed whether you have found the culprits. And, by the way, may I inquire if you've determined who caused Louise Higginbotham's accident and the disappearance of Andy Harris?"

Bundy looked down his nose.

"Andy Harris is hardly any of your concern or do you somehow know more about him than you are willing to admit?"

We bounced the ball back and forth some more but in the end Bundy stuffed his notebook into a sleek leather briefcase and got up. When he was about to disappear down the terrace steps Noelle jumped up and followed him. Mel glowered at them as Noelle grabbed Bundy's arm and their heads came together briefly while he talked into her ear. She looked back over her shoulder when Mel got up, let go of Bundy's arm, and returned to the table.

"Why do you always fawn over that guy," Mel said and let his arm hang loose although Noelle twined hers around it. "Let's keep out of it, this is none of our business."

"Don't be such an old fuss-pot." She beamed at him. "I only wanted to make sure he didn't mean all that stuff he told Jamie. He didn't. He just gets all official and stiff, he hasn't been a chief inspector that long."

"You needn't intercede on my behalf," I said. "I'm perfectly capable of taking care of guys like Bundy. But thank you for keeping me company and thank you for the lovely dinner."

"Well," Noelle said. "Looks like you can manage without us now. Mel, we'd better get home."

"Did you leave a cigarette burning?" Mel whispered when he hugged me goodbye.

"Did I leave a cigarette burning?" I repeated "Of course not. Did you ever see me smoke?"

"Sorry."

Sorry was right. My cottage was burned to the ground, my paintings melted down, my Saks Fifth Avenue wardrobe, my Wilson tennis racket and my suitcase in ashes. I patted my backpack gratefully. It hugged the cerise sun dress in salute to my lack of vanity. As a result, I still had my passport, ticket, cash, and traveler's checks, my cell phone, a small notebook, a Parker pen, a comb, a lipstick, and one Tootsie roll.

I watched them depart—arguing all the way to the parking lot—and felt relieved at the thought of leaving them behind forever. I moved to the terrace rail and looked down towards my cottage. Water had been doused on the surrounding trees to prevent sparks from igniting but the fire looked as if it had been contained. A sad wisp of smoke rose from the black ashes.

I went inside to the reception and found they had given me room 212 in the main building. The receptionist assured me that everything possible was being done to make me comfortable. On my way up the curved staircase to the second floor I realized I still hadn't told Mel and Noelle that I would be leaving Sunday. And I hadn't told Bundy.

Some kind soul—could it be Jeanette?—had supplied me with a toothbrush and toothpaste in addition to the customary shampoos, lotions, and soaps. A cotton robe was laid out on the bed and I decided it was meant to be my new pyjamas. I washed out my only underwear and hung up my only dress.

When I had tucked myself into bed I lay there in a panic suddenly realizing that my books had gone up in flames. I ended up reading the hotel magazine from cover to cover needlessly perusing ads about scuba diving, tennis, and biking tours but paying special attention to the ad from the boutique in the hotel. I would have to go there first thing in the morning.

My last thought was that I must keep away from Bundy from now on.

CHAPTER 18

I was the first and only customer shown in when a slim and very petite person opened the doors to the boutique.

"You're the woman from the burned cottage," she declared.

I've gained notoriety, I thought. Again.

"Unfortunately, yes," I said. "And I desperately need a few pieces of clothing."

"Right." She looked at me doubtfully. "I am afraid, Madam, I do not have anything in such a large size."

"I'm only a 12," I said defensively and felt my shoulders droop and my spine shrink trying to become a size 8—or I should be so lucky—a 6.

I went behind the curtain which paraded as a dressing room and tried on the largest bikini I could find on the rack. On me, it was the epitome of itsy-bitsy and consisted of diagonal red and white stripes making me look as if I was wearing the flag, with stars hidden God knew where. What the heck, I thought, as I paid the equivalent of eighty dollars. The sea would disguise me. Then for good measure I added a bright red wrap and a bottle of suntan lotion.

"You look lovely, Madam," Miss Helpful declared as I walked out feeling less than glamorous dressed in skimpy jeans, a very tight tee, and a pre-shrunk cotton shirt, carrying a canvas tote with the rest of my new stuff. I could, of course, have gone to duty-free heaven on Broad Street in Bridgetown and spent some serious money in designer boutiques but I didn't see the sense in that. The discomfort would be temporary

At noon Andrew called me to say that Louise was home and would like to see me.

"But please don't stay too long," he said. "She's apt to overdo things, thinks she's stronger than she is." Well, I thought, or maybe she's just as strong as she thinks she is. As I had learned, Louise was no slouch.

As I'd half expected she took the news of my imminent departure well. When I told her I had changed my return ticket to the following day, she immediately concentrated on business and wanted to make sure I was all squared away.

"You will be busy now," Louise said. "I'm afraid you won't have time to help me with the investigation."

"The investigation?"

"Yes, I cannot rest until I know everything about the last months of Elizabeth's life in England. I don't even know for sure where she stayed and where she's buried."

"Couldn't you just ask Hugh Mattson?" I asked.

"He returned two days ago and immediately went sailing."

"But surely you'll see him at some point, or you could ask Amaryllis?" I said.

"Amaryllis says she doesn't know. She says the death certificate is in probate court and the records are sealed."

"Strange, but of course I don't know the regulations here. You do know Elizabeth went to Hertfordshire, don't you? That should narrow it down some. They must have some central archives for vital statistics."

"I don't think she had ever been to Hertfordshire before

but maybe her relatives from Surrey had moved there. Elizabeth never really talked about them. They were not at all close. I do so much wish you could investigate this for me." Louise sniffled. "I can't think of anyone who would do a better job."

"Well, thank you." I looked at Louise and wondered how deep into this I should get considering the physical distance between Barbados and Maryland. "I could certainly get someone on the case in England. I should be able to find out about the place of death."

"But my dear, that is simply marvelous. How will you do that? Or aren't I supposed to ask?"

I had a funny feeling that Louise now saw herself as a character in a Miss Marple mystery. I jotted down Elizabeth's date and place of birth, the date of her departure for England, the date of her death and burial.

When I left half an hour later Louise was looking pale and exhausted but her grip on my hand spoke of strength and tenacity.

In the early morning hours I slipped into my new tiny bikini and wrap and set off for the beach. A solitary fisherman stood close to the shore waist-high in water, his velvet skin glistening in the sun with a thousand diamonds. He stretched out his right arm and—with the center cord between his teeth—cast the net, setting it free to float above the surface. After it landed gently on the waves, the shadow lay there a moment before it disappeared.

I had my last swim.

I could have by-passed the burned-out cottage on my way back to the hotel but before I knew it I was in the garden on blackened ground surrounded by seared tree trunks. A few wooden posts—charred and brittle—stood where the porch had been. I knew I wouldn't find anything but couldn't help looking towards the empty space that used to be the bedroom. The rubble was sodden with water and black soot and the collapsed roof covered the entire floor. I wondered briefly whether my insurance company would consider this an act of God or ante up without complaint.

I had picked up my tote getting ready for the airport when the phone rang.

It was Louise. She sounded completely recovered and with something in her voice which I couldn't immediately place.

"Jamie, dear, you remember when we went to Hugh's library and you stuffed an airline folder into my handbag?"

"Yes?"

"Well, my dear, I just had a look through the folder and you will not believe what I found."

"*What?*"

"My dear. I found three boarding pass stubs. Two with Hugh's name and one for Elizabeth."

"Well, yes," I said. "You would, wouldn't you. Hugh must have had two because he returned from England. But Elizabeth didn't use hers."

"Not quite, my dear. You see, the three stubs were not for the trip London-Barbados. They were for travel between London and Copenhagen."

CHAPTER 19

The sugarcane fields sloped away and receded through a mist of powdery clouds as the jet soared upwards and carried me away from Barbados.

I have a reputation for traveling light—to a ridiculous degree, according to Topsy—but this time I had certainly outdone myself. At the airport I had been asked rather pointedly if that was all I was carrying and when I said, yes, my suitcase burned up in a hotel fire, I received some unbelieving looks.

I settled down to read the book I'd bought at the airport—an English romance novel which I abandoned after struggling through the first ten pages. The breaking point came when the incredibly handsome hero said to the incredibly beautiful heroine, that he worshiped her rose petal body.

I stared out the window into the blue void and played out my conversation with Louise for the umpteenth time.

Hadn't Hugh Mattson told me distinctly that he had not been to Denmark since he was a child? Why would he have gone out of his way to lie about it? Was Elizabeth's missing stub sufficient reason to suspect that only Hugh Mattson had returned to London? Hugh Mattson hadn't struck me as an overly fastidious man. To wit, his desk had been a mess. Would a man like that have kept all his stubs? After all, stubs were tiny, people left them in their seat pocket or simply threw them away when the trip was over.

The fact remained that one boarding pass stub—and a significant one, at that—was missing. I had to ask myself the next question. What if Elizabeth had really never left Denmark?

I hurried through passport control in Miami, handed in my customs form, by-passed luggage claim since I had nothing to claim, and caught my connection to Washington.

In Bethesda, I felt my spirits lift at the sight of my Cape Cod style house. I had acquired it when Topsy and I started our travel agency and decided to remodel it. The agency occupies the first floor and I have the two upper stories with an entrance from the side of the house.

I looked around my living room which had that forlorn appearance it gets when I'm away. My only fern had withered for lack of Topsy's attention and I dashed to the kitchen in search of water. After dousing the plant vigorously and mopping up the pool which quickly gathered on the floor, I popped a frozen dinner in the microwave, poured a glass of white Zinfandel and turned on the first of a dozen messages on the answering machine.

After skipping several marketing calls I got to Bob Makowski's short message.

"Hi, Jamie, it's me, Bob. Topsy told me you're returning early, sorry about that. How about lunch downtown on Tuesday. Call me."

I fast-forwarded through several more marketing calls until I heard my mother's voice. She doesn't waste time on superfluous talk either so her message was brief and to the point.

"Topsy tells me you'll be home Sunday evening. Do come over for dinner Monday night if you're free. Call me."

Then I heard Mel's voice through a series of beeps and burps.

"Hi, sweetheart," he said, and since when were we on sweetheart terms? "I'll be in New York next month. I'll call you. Ciao." I laughed and suddenly missed the sun and the beach, the coral reefs under the turquoise water, and even *Mauby* and the flying fish.

Then it was Topsy's turn, she had called Saturday.

"My Savior," she said. "Hope it wasn't too, too distressing for you to leave your vacation paradise and come to my rescue. We brought Julie to her dorm from the hospital this morning, she has a brace around her neck—the doctor insisted—but, thank God, she's fine. I'm going to pamper her for a couple of days and then I'll be home. Hopefully by Friday. I'll be in touch. Love and kisses, mmmmm. Oh, and I'm having people for dinner next Saturday, please say you'll come."

She's planning to fix me up with some impossible man, I thought.

I was in the office downstairs at eight Monday morning getting a good hour's work done before Kristy showed up fifteen minutes late with her coffee and donut from the bakery across the street. Topsy had left a pile of disorganized papers for me to sort through and this took me until well after lunch. Then I tackled the files our perfidious Margo had abandoned. It was four before I got to my own clients and after six before I called my mother to take a rain check on dinner until Tuesday.

I had Kristy put in an hour's overtime to photocopy schedules for the tours to Peru and Bolivia which were scheduled to begin two weeks hence. Before leaving, she pouted her way through stuffing envelopes and assembling travel kits for the first twenty tour members.

I answered a slew of e-mails, glanced through incoming mail, and at ten staggered upstairs. By now I had decided quite definitely to turn down Louise's request to go to Copenhagen on the grounds that I could think of no grounds.

CHAPTER 20

The next day I left my sleek new Jaguar in a parking lot on E Street and set out in the direction of the Teutonic gray FBI building. A tall emaciated panhandler appeared out of nowhere, veered straight into my path and held out a grubby hand. I gave him the change in my pocket: a dollar fifty.

I entered Pennsylvania Avenue where the lunch hour traffic moved by sedately in six lanes, and speeded up until I rounded the Navy Memorial and found the coffee shop where I spotted Bob Makowski already in place. He sat facing the door with his back to the wall, a defensive position dating back to his days at the Bureau. As usual, he looked full of unexpended vigor.

He bounced from his seat as soon as I entered, pointed to two full trays showing he had my lunch ready, and waved me forward in his customary impatient fashion. I could tell from his upbeat demeanor that he'd just come from one of his periodic conferences with his old pals in the Criminal Division on the fifth floor. After fifteen years on the job he had resigned to set up his own agency—successfully, as it turned out. I had joined his firm soon after getting my master's in criminology from Georgetown University and obtained my license as a private investigator after my required three-year stint under his tutelage. When I decided to become a peaceful travel agent a couple of years ago Bob was disappointed and still persuades me to take on occasional jobs for him.

I hurried to the table, peeling off my jacket as I pushed my way around tables, all occupied, to sit down opposite him—with my back to the door, naturally, but then we don't have the same hang-ups. Bob, a meat and potatoes man, had a steak sandwich and had gotten me a vegetarian roll-up. We both had iced tea, this being an alcohol-free establishment.

"Too bad you had to return early because of Topsy. She also said you'd run into some 'issues' in Barbados." Bob bit into his sandwich and eyed me suspiciously. "What issues?"

I took my time chewing on my roll-up and sipping tea.

"Well? Don't just sit there looking innocent. What happened?"

"What happened?" I said, and put down my glass. "I rescued one guy from drowning then I found another already drowned, I got pushed off a cliff with my rented mountain bike and had to slide to the bottom clutching at thorny bushes, and two days ago my cottage burned down, I lost three lovely Haitian paintings in addition to my clothes, I returned looking like an orphan in skimpy jeans, a tight tee, and a wrinkled shirt, carrying my borrowed toothbrush in a tote. And here I am."

Bob had stopped eating which meant I really had his attention.

"You're kidding, right? No," he answered himself, "of course you're not. You couldn't keep out of trouble and just have a quiet vacation. I should've known. Now lay it out for me."

"The thing is, Louise Higginbotham wants me to find out what really happened to her childhood friend, Elizabeth Mattson. She wants me to go to Denmark."

I gave him all the details as if making an investigative report. When I finished, Bob shook his head.

"What's so peculiar about them taking a side trip to Copenhagen?" he said.

"Because I remember distinctly that Hugh Mattson said he'd never been to Denmark. He lied. And the stub for Elizabeth's return to London was missing. After Hugh Mattson very reluctantly gave Louise an address for Elizabeth in England, Louise wrote but never got a reply."

"That doesn't mean Hugh didn't hear from his wife. After all, Louise is not family," Bob said.

"She's probably closer than a sister," I said, forgetting that this had been my own argument not too long ago.

"And, not to be too contrary, where would Hugh have hidden the body in Copenhagen?"

"You've seen enough of this kind of thing to know it's entirely possible for a determined killer," I said, feeling my stubborn streak raise it's head.

Bob's face revealed his skeptical, although amused, thoughts.

"Now that's what I call fanciful," he said. "He would have taken quite a risk. The body could have been found and identified just by her foreign clothing."

"Murderers take risks," I said. "He could have disposed of her naked body somewhere and who would have connected that to a foreigner? Especially if enough time had elapsed."

"Okay, okay."

Bob finished his sandwich, gulped down the rest of his iced tea, and pushed back his chair so he could teeter on its two back legs.

"People don't keep their boarding pass stubs. I don't," he said.

"No, you wouldn't 'cause you're sloppy, but *I* do, at least until I get my frequent flier statement."

"Then why don't you check with the airlines," he said. "See if she returned to England."

"Tried that already, but I have no buddies at Scandinavian Airlines and they became very uppity when I insisted. Some kind of Viking scruples about confidentiality. I can't budge them."

"Then do as Louise asks. Go over there."

"What?"

"Go over there. Haven't you always said you wanted to see Copenhagen?"

"No, I've never said that. What's more, my mother has never said that. She left when she was eighteen and has never been back. I asked her once, and she said, home is where the heart is, and her heart is in America."

"Isn't that a little strange? She—and consequently you—must have family over there. You're an investigator, haven't you ever wondered about them?"

"Oh, well, maybe once in a while. But never enough to do anything about it."

"Now you have an excuse. Go find Elizabeth."

"On the strength of a missing boarding pass stub?"

"Don't you have travel agency business to conduct over there?"

"Nope. Topsy has Scandinavian tours covered. I'm the South American expert, remember? Why are you pushing this?"

"Don't know, really." Bob tapped the side of his nose. "Just a feeling."

"How can you have a feeling about this. You don't know enough details." I was getting stubborn. I didn't see the point in dragging off to a far country on so little evidence. "Help me out here, instead. You have that guy in London who traced the run-away teenager last year. All I need is to find out where Elizabeth died and was buried. Then Louise will let it rest."

"It can take a while," Bob said as we left the coffee shop. "This is not an official request. I'll depend on the goodwill of this guy who doesn't even owe me."

"That's all right. I have time, I'll wait."

"You're not returning to Barbados to finish your vacation, and keep up that tan, when Topsy comes back?"

"No, it has lost its attraction, thank you very much. Where are you parked?"

"Right here," Bob said, stopped at a meter and philosophically removed the parking ticket flapping in the wind under the windshield wiper.

I returned to the agency to find Kristy still out to lunch. I had a message from Louise and she was at her desk at the agency in Bridgetown when I called her back.

"I've been thinking and thinking since you left," she said. "I will pay your fee, get you a ticket to Copenhagen, and take care of your expenses," she said in a harsh voice. "Will you do it for me? Will you find out what happened to Elizabeth over there?"

I told her about Bob Makowski and his promise to investigate in England.

"We should wait for those results first," I said, but Louise was adamant.

"I cannot bear to be inactive any longer. I have the most terrible premonitions. Please say you will go."

I meant to tell her that it was the longest shot I'd ever encountered in an investigation but, somehow, I didn't. I could see it now. If nothing came of my investigation in Copenhagen Louise would want me to continue in England. Please let Bob's guy in London hurry up, I prayed silently. I hoped Louise didn't hear the heavy sighing at my end.

"Of course I will help you, Louise," I said.

When I hung up I sat there for a while reciting to myself the next moves in the game before I turned back to the work at hand.

At four, Kristy declared she was feeling unwell—no doubt yesterday's overtime had taken its toll—and she left. I saw her cross the street to the bakery.

At five I closed the agency and headed to my mother's house.

CHAPTER 21

My mother has lived in this three-story red brick townhouse in Georgetown since my father—who was twenty years her senior—died. She is a partner in a small law firm in Washington, D.C. and says she intends to practice until she's carried out.

She met me on the doorstep and exclaimed at the yellow tulips I brought her, as if I didn't always. Yellow is her favorite color, as it is mine. When I sat in her living room looking at her several inherited pieces of furniture it suddenly occurred to me that I'd never bothered to ask where they'd come from. They had simply been a part of my childhood home. But, more to the point, my mother had never volunteered the information.

"Where did your writing desk come from?" I asked. It stood against the far wall flanked by two Victorian dining chairs not unlike those I'd seen recently in Louise Higginbotham's house in Barbados. My yellow tulips now stood there in a round glass vase. There were framed photos of me as a child with my pony and one with my parents at my graduation. It was as if my mother's life had started with my father and me in America.

"It was my mother's." My mother looked as if that was the end of the subject. "What can I get you? We're having white wine with dinner. Would you like to start now?"

I nodded and when we sat with our wine glasses I said: "What was she like, your mother? And your father? Do you realize the only thing I know about them is that they died when you were sixteen. That must have been so hard for you. Where did you live the next two years?"

My mother looked above my head as if into the distant past with such a pained expression that I was sorry I'd asked.

"You don't have to talk about it if you don't want to," I said hurriedly. "It's just that I've suddenly developed a professional interest in Denmark."

My mother put down her empty wine glass and motioned me to the dining room.

"Come, tell me about it over dinner," she said. "Poached salmon with new potatoes in dill sauce. We'll fill up our glasses. How lovely to spend a long evening together, just the two of us."

I gave her a succinct account of my Barbados adventure—excluding the most perilous aspects of the rugged East Coast experience—placing the emphasis on Elizabeth Mattson.

"Now," I concluded, "the suspicion is that she may have disappeared in Denmark instead of dying in England. Bob has promised to get in touch with an operative in London but it'll take time. And he's actually pushing for me to go to Denmark to follow the tenuous lead of a missing boarding pass stub."

We had strawberry shortcake and ice-cream followed by decaf cappuccino, and went back to the living room after I'd helped stack the dishwasher.

"After my parents died our house was sold and their things put in storage," my mother said quite without preliminaries as if I'd just asked my question. "I lived for two years with my father's cousin, Leonora. She had a daughter my age. Her name was Margrethe. When I was eighteen I went to study in Washington and after I married your father I brought my parents' antiques over."

"Didn't you have aunts and uncles?"

"No, my father was an only child." My mother smiled. "Just like I was, and like you are. And he had only two first cousins. It was a small family all around. And my mother had no one."

"And you've lost touch with Leonora?" I couldn't imagine why we'd never had this conversation.

"Every five years or so I would hear from her and then I gather she must have died. Margrethe never wrote, and we lost touch. And that's all, really. Not a very exciting story."

"You said your mother had no one. What do you mean?"

"My mother was Swedish. She was born in 1920 into an important family. Landed aristocracy, you might say.

"What?" I exclaimed. "Landed aristocracy? I can't believe this is the first I hear of this. You mean, your mother was of royal blood?"

"No, no. Her great-grandfather was knighted in the early1800s but that didn't make the family of royal blood."

I was still impressed and, I freely admit, somewhat dazzled to learn of my hitherto unknown distinguished background.

My mother continued as if I wasn't in the room.

"My mother," she said, "was brought up on their country estate south of Stockholm. I gather she was both impetuous and willful. When she met my father—who was an engineering student from Copenhagen completing his foreign internship at the state railways in Stockholm—she decided he was the man for her. After several clandestine meetings they eloped to Copenhagen—by train, of course—and were married there. My mother was 19, my father 22."

"What happened then?"

"My mother was punished for making such an unsuitable marriage and was forevermore disowned by her parents, her siblings, and other respectable folk."

"And they never reconciled?"

"I don't believe so. At least my mother never talked about them. I only learned all this from my father who was not as reticent as she." My mother smiled. "I suppose I take after her. I'm sorry I've never told you all this before. You really deserve to know. But, somehow, I put it all behind me when I married your father. And, truly, it all seems so far away and long ago."

"Then your mother didn't bring her writing desk with her from Sweden?"

"No, the writing desk was given to her by my father's mother." She laughed. "You'll be losing track of all this pretty soon."

She got up and went to the old writing desk, opened one of the little drawers, and brought out a single photograph.

"Here I am," she said. "With my parents, Leonora, her husband, and Margrethe. No photos of my mother's family. You'll have to picture them in your imagination. No doubt fine looking, tall Vikings. Not unlike you, probably."

When we said goodbye at the front door my mother said: "I'll write to Margrethe. She may still live in her parents' old house. Just in case you decide to go to Copenhagen to trace Elizabeth Mattson, I mean. Goodnight, my dear. And next time you take a vacation try a desert island."

Late Thursday afternoon Topsy called me at the office just as Kristy left early due to a sudden attack of ennui. Why did I have the distinct feeling she wouldn't last much longer in our employ?

"Just got back from California and, thank the Lord, Julie is all right," Topsy enthused, "but I'm too, too exhausted to come to the office tomorrow. I'll be there on Monday. But first, I'll see you for dinner Saturday night."

I cringed and tried silently to formulate my reply. Before I could get it out, Topsy wailed in my ear.

"You're thinking of an excuse, aren't you?"

"No, it's not an excuse, it's for real."

"Oh, Jamie. And I had planned the loveliest surprise for you."

"What?"

"Archibald Brewster will be there. He's back in town and he asked about you."

"And what did you tell him?"

"I told him you'd like to see him." Topsy's voice came across very small.

"You did what?"

"Well, you do, I know you do. Want to see him, I mean."

"Topsy, I'm off to Copenhagen Saturday morning."

"What *can* you mean?"

She kept me on the phone until I'd explained the entire story and then some.

"But what do I tell Brewster?" she said at the end.

"Just tell him hello."

"Okay, okay, I'll tell him to call you when you return."

"I said, just tell him hello."

CHAPTER 22

Clad in a '70s muumuu, she had red apple cheeks, large feet in Birkenstock sandals, and held aloft a sign which proclaimed she was in search of USA—*Jamie Prescott.*

Who's this, I thought. Too young to be second cousin Margrethe. Or was Margrethe my mother's second cousin once removed? Then this might be someone twice removed from my mother. What did it make her to me? Thrice removed? I felt dizzy.

Because of the time constraint of my trip to Denmark—four days from the day I decided until the day I departed—my mother had found Margrethe's phone number in Copenhagen, and, having confused the time difference, surprised her one very late night and sprung my imminent arrival on her. Putting all this behind me, I approached the woman with the enticing sign.

I disappeared into the folds of her muumuu in a gigantic embrace. My nostrils filled with whiffs of stale cigarette smoke, exotic herbs and—could it be?—grass. My eyes itched and so did my nose and, irresistibly, I sneezed. I was partly released and tottered a few steps sideways, my arm in a steadying grip.

"Hi, there," boomed a voice. "My mother sent me to get you."

"Well, hi, yourself. Who are you?"

"I am Birgit, your second cousin once removed, or something."

That still didn't explain exactly who she was, but at least we seemed to be related. I must admit I didn't feel any kinship at all. More like confusion.

She grabbed a hold of my suitcase, rolled it along on a dizzying journey between trolleys and tourists and led me through several doors which opened and shut electronically about us as we proceeded towards a roomy parking area just off the arrival hall.

We stopped next to an ancient Peugeot. My suitcase was dumped unceremoniously on the back seat—I would discover later that the trunk of the car was permanently stuck—and I went into the passenger seat.

Birgit placed her body in the driver's seat, sank back with a great big sigh and lit up the first of the one thousand cigarettes she would inhale during our next weeks together. She blew out a slow stream of debilitating fumes. I went for the handle to roll down my window but it was like the trunk—stuck. I had no choice but to become a second-hand smoker. Horrible visions sprang up in my mind of charred lung tissue and racking coughs. I thought with some relief of the non-smoking hotel room which awaited me in central Copenhagen.

But that wasn't where we were headed.

Birgit crunched into gear and we swept out of *Kastrup* airport towards the center of town, across a draw bridge and past a canal lined with great looking old houses painted red, green, blue, and sunshine yellow, with roofs of black-glazed tile. Past churches with complicated spires and through streets with red brick apartment buildings. People—seemingly with all their earthly belongings in packs on their backs—pedaled away on bicycles, bent purposefully over the handlebars. Otherwise, the streets looked deserted, at least to my eyes.

"Rush hour," Birgit mumbled, as we passed one bus and a car. When she said "You know," and bent down to explore the floor under her seat with her right hand while steering with her left, I thought for one fanciful moment she was about to pull a Louise Higginbotham and give me tidbits of information about sights in Copenhagen. Instead she came up from the depth of the car with a cell phone.

"You know, it's illegal to talk on this thing while you drive," she said, punched in a number and started talking in a low murmur. I couldn't catch a single syllable.

"Our Savior's Church," she suddenly said in the middle of her monotonous sounding telephone conversation and pointed to a spiraled tower topped by a globe and a tiny gold figure with a banner. "You can climb to the top if you wish."

"I might do just that," I said but I don't think she heard me.

"I'm taking you the scenic route." Birgit abruptly abandoned her illegal cell phone conversation. "Business. Sorry. I'm working on an article about the developments in Christiania. It's over there."

She pointed towards a collection of unkempt houses and low walls covered with straggling ivy and graffiti. So, this was Hippieland, which I'd heard described somewhere as an anarchistic abode for pot-smoking, anti-social, protesting youth. I was not very surprised to hear Birgit say: "I used to live there," and for her to send the run-down eyesore fond glances.

"This is so much fun," she said. "Imagine finding an American relative. Such a surprise."

"I was surprised, too," I said. "My mother left Denmark when she was 18. I'd never even heard of you."

"I've been to New York several times," Birgit said. "A pity I didn't know about you then. Well, next time. We'll find out in a jiffy what has happened to your missing person and then I'll show you the Copenhagen night life."

"I may not have time for that," I said and coughed up a lungful of her smoke. I thought she shot me a suspicious glance as she ground out her cigarette, an action which caused old ashes to descend from the ashtray and settle on my shoes.

Birgit put her foot on the brakes and I jerked forward.

"We're going to my mother's house before I take you to your hotel. She insisted she must meet you the minute you set foot on Danish soil. I'm sorry I couldn't have spared you that, you won't enjoy it, but at least you'll get it over with right away. But first, let's see if the Queen is at home."

"The flag is up," Birgit said, when we had made a detour to the four identical palaces which composed the *Amalienborg* castle. She bumped the car across a large square paved in granite cobble cubes, the kind that last centuries. "That means the queen is in residence."

For one crazy moment I thought we were actually going to visit. Instead, I said, "I would have thought that as a former anarchist you would not be a Royalist."

"But of course, I am!" Birgit looked scandalized. "That has nothing to do with anything."

It didn't? My confusion intensified.

We drove on in silence backtracking across the center of town until Birgit announced that we were now in the section of town called *Fredriksberg*. The four-story buildings on the main street were similar to those I had seen on our way in from the airport, lined with small shops.

We stopped on a quiet side street in front of a large villa. It was partially hidden behind a well-manicured hedge. Just under the roof sat an oval stone plaque with the year 1910. The street number, 27, was on a white enameled sign on a small chainlink gate.

"We're here," Birgit kicked her car door open in preference to using the handle. I did the same to mine and wondered briefly what would happen if she ever needed to get out in an emergency. A good thing I'd have my own rental car as of tomorrow morning. When we stood on the sidewalk I made a move to retrieve my suitcase from the back seat, but Birgit stopped me.

"Just leave it," she said. "No need to drag it in. It'll be perfectly safe in the car."

When Birgit rang the bell we were greeted immediately by a tall woman in her early sixties. She wore a straight black skirt and a white blouse. Disconcertingly, my mother's blue eyes looked at me from her unfamiliar face.

CHAPTER 23

So, this was Margrethe. My mother's kin and yet so different. This woman was loosely built where my mother was lean. Her hair was straight where my mother's was curly. Her nails were cut short where my mother's were manicured.

"It's so terribly thrilling to meet you. I'm your mother's second cousin once removed—at least I think that's what it is," she said in clipped BBC English. "Please come in and let me introduce you to my other daughter. Lise, say hello to Jamie Prescott, your American twin."

Lise appeared at Margrethe's elbow and I should feel flattered because Lise was a spectacular blonde, about fifteen years my junior, with an athletic body. The shape of her face with its straight nose, full lips and flawless skin did, indeed, resemble my own. Her hair, though, was several shades lighter than mine, possibly helped along by hydrogen peroxide, and when she smiled I felt the resemblance fade.

Her teeth just weren't as good as mine.

"Hi, there," she said in a New York drawl. "Nice to meet you. I've just returned from three years at Parson's School of Design. Loved it. I'll go back as soon as possible." I thought she eyed her mother defiantly.

Margrethe led me into the square foyer.

"And this is Lillian—your mother's other second cousin once removed. She has an antique shop in the northern part of town." Lillian was plump under a heavily embroidered blouse. She was stuck in the time warp of her early youth with bangs grazing her eyelids, her long hair gray at the roots and yellow at the tips.

"Did I hear someone say you're looking for a missing black woman from Barbados?" she said in the same clipped accent as Margrethe's.

"I'm afraid one small feather is turning into five hens," I said, barely preventing myself from brushing the hair out of her eyes. "It's true I'm looking for a missing woman and she's from Barbados, but she isn't black."

"Oh, really? I thought Barbados was a black country. Not that we don't have black people here, well, more like Mediterranean types, especially around where *I* live, but on the whole a black person would stand out in Denmark. That'll make your search more difficult. How did she disappear?"

"We'll hear all about it over lunch," Margrethe said. "Here, I want you to meet Birgit's chap, Hans. He's a student of sociology. In his seventh year." She couldn't quite keep the asperity out of her voice.

Blue eyes twinkled merrily in a huge face surrounded by a reddish Viking beard. A large paw enveloped my hand and Hans showed me his pointy white teeth. I felt like Little Red Riding Hood. He put his arm around Birgit and scratched his beard thoughtfully.

"Just now I am taking a break for a year or so. I may travel half a year in India."

"What will you do there?" I asked.

"I will experience a third world culture. It'll be cheap." He looked at me hopefully. "I'll meet interesting people."

"And," I said, "will you write your thesis on some aspect of Indian culture?"

"I haven't thought about it."

"Ahh."

I felt the energy level in the room decrease by several degrees and the culture gap widening.

"Oscar, my husband, is at the office," Margrethe said, and urged me through three handsome old rooms with high ceilings, elaborate moldings, and crystal chandeliers. Silver was on display everywhere. The windows were hung with heavy curtains, and ceramic pots with well-tended plants adorned the wide window-sills. The pictures on the walls were unremarkable except for the heavy gilded frames.

The dining room table was set with crystal glasses, silver flatware, and Royal Danish fluted blue. The *smørrebrød* stood on serving platters down the middle of the table. Dark rye bread with mountains of tiny shrimp and thin slices of lemon. Pickled herring. Slabs of pale liver paste with red beets. Catered, I thought. No one except professionals could possibly have created these masterpieces of open-faced sandwiches.

"Mother has slaved through the night," Birgit said. "She always goes overboard."

Lise and Birgit sat across from one another. I studied them surreptitiously and observed, not for the first time, how dissimilar sisters can be.

Lise waved her fork in the air and addressed no one in particular.

"The public toilets in the town hall square."

"Lise," her mother said with ice in her voice and sent a warning signal towards Birgit. "Please. Not at the table."

Too late. Birgit, answering to a well-honed irresistible impulse, rose to the bait.

"What do you mean, 'public toilets'?"

"The black monstrosity in town hall square. Wouldn't it have made more sense to hide a bus terminal behind the central train station?"

Birgit waved her fork.

"Who cares," she said and speared a shrimp. "It's just a building."

"Ah," said Lise. "So you agree it cannot be called architecture."

"Girls, girls," their mother wailed with an apoplectic glance at me.

"What do *you* think?" Lise said to me. "Have you seen it?"

As a matter of fact, I had—when Birgit drove us across the town hall square—and had wondered what it could be. A black rectangular box as incongruous in its surroundings as I. M. Pei's pyramid at the Louvre.

I took the coward's way out and turned to Margrethe.

"*Skål*," she said. She lifted her glass of akvavit in my direction and I realized too late that I'd triggered the schnapps response. I had no choice but to drink. Heat invaded my chest, and I struggled to see her through my blurred vision. They all laughed and the public toilets were forgotten.

"It's such a pity your mother and I lost touch. She came to my wedding just before she left, you know. I had just turned 18."

No, I didn't know. If Margrethe and my mother were the same age, I thought, then Margrethe must have had her children much later. I judged Birgit to be in her early thirties and Lise in her mid-twenties.

"It was a great tragedy. Your grandparents went to Switzerland and they were killed in that horrible train crash."

"I didn't know that was how they died."

"Your mother felt guilty because she hadn't accompanied them," Margrethe said and handed me a platter.

And then she came to America, I thought, and created a new life for herself.

Coffee was served in the sitting room and I found myself next to Lillian, the antique shop owner. I stirred my gold-rimmed demi-tasse with a dainty enameled teaspoon and emptied it in one gulp. Lillian laughed.

"You need another serving." She got up to pour me more black coffee. I reached for the sugar. "Tell me about your missing woman," she said.

"She arrived here several months ago and it appears that she never left."

"How strange. Will you try the hospitals?"

"Possibly," I said weakly, thinking of the many months I would need to cover that possibility.

"Are you interested in antiques?" She dismissed the subject of private investigation and when I said yes, she handed me her card. "Here's my address and phone number at the store. I'm in most weekdays at ten, just drop by. On Saturdays you'll find me at the flea market."

After coffee I looked around for Birgit and Hans and discovered them when I glanced out the window. They were on the lawn pulsing away furiously. I walked out on the front steps.

"Jamie," Birgit scowled. "We had to have a smoke. My mother doesn't allow it in the house. She has asthma."

"Yes, I noticed the absence of cigarettes."

"This is for you," Birgit said when we were back inside. "The telephone number to the police station. Your mother said you wanted to look at all of Zealand but I think that'll be a bit much."

I stuffed the card in my bag.

"My cell phone number is on the card. Come, we'll take you to your hotel now," Birgit said. "I'm sorry I can't accompany you anywhere this week but I have a deadline for my Christiania article."

At least someone was working towards a deadline in this century.

At the door Margrethe handed me a photograph.

"I don't know how it ended up with me," she said. I've kept it all these years. It's your grandmother's birthplace in Sweden. If I remember correctly the name was *Bokhamra*."

It was an early aerial photo of a stately manor house set in the midst of vast fields and forests. I felt my investigative juices stirring.

Margrethe embraced me warmly and at that moment I suddenly felt we were family.

Birgit and Hans delivered me to my hotel on the Hans Christian Andersen Boulevard. In my room I stripped down to nothing, threw my smoke-infested clothes in a dry-cleaning bag, rinsed out underwear and socks, and shampooed my hair vigorously under a hot shower.

As a compensation I felt was due me, the hotel was quite lovely and reminded me vaguely of the Left Bank in Paris. I had a corner room courtesy of management in deference to my travel agent status. The furniture was Danish modern. A black sofa snuggled into a small niche. A teak coffee table with a tray contained the trappings of a continental breakfast *sens* the breakfast. A bay window was framed by red floor to ceiling curtains.

I looked out across the rooftops of Copenhagen, at the solid tower of the town hall, at the roofs and chimneys of the surrounding buildings, at the numerous spires almost obscured by the mist of the early night.

But instead of enjoying the moment I had a sudden panic attack at the thought of Elizabeth Granger-Farley Mattson. Had she been out there? What had happened to her?

CHAPTER 24

"Just a moment," or, as they say in Copenhagen, "*lige et øjeblik*"—pronounced "lee-at-oh-yeah-blech"—became the leitmotif of my first day as an alien private investigator.

'Everyone speaks English,' had been the refrain which misled me into thinking I could actually do this on my own. I called the police station at nine in the morning, under the assumption that the working day would start no later, and got a recorded message which I did not understand. On my third attempt I thought I caught the word "eleven"— sounding like "*ellll-ve*"—and figured that the public would be dealt with by that hour. In the meantime it was only nine-thirty.

I ordered room service and, having soon devoured rolls and real butter washed down with plenty of coffee with thick cream, spent the next half hour trying to offset the effects of my indulgence by exercising. At precisely eleven I was back on the line explaining to the operator that I needed to speak to a criminal investigator. I was greeted by the first in a series of the just-a-moment syndrome. I was put on hold.

I walked with the phone to the bay window and took in the daylight sight of the roofs and towers I'd seen only obscurely last night. I looked down at the town hall square at Lise's public toilets.

I waited. No music. Just a profound silence. Had I been disconnected? Was someone in the dark desperately trying to find an English-speaker? Was the operator on her break having coffee and a Danish? Did they have a criminal investigations unit, at all?

I gave up and took the stairs down, two at a time, to the front desk. Ghita, the receptionist, spoke to me sweetly in English, listened to my harried explanation, called the number I gave her, mumbled into the receiver, laughed, mumbled some more, nodded her head, wrote down something, said '*tusind tak*' which even I recognized as 'a thousand thanks,' hung up, and handed me her note.

"Here you are. This is the name of an investigator, Kriminalassistent Mogens Hansen, and I will now show you how to get there." And she highlighted the route to the police station on my map.

I thanked her profusely, hoped she would be on permanent call at the front desk, and set out on my quest. It was eleven-thirty. The police station was housed in a nondescript, low-slung, concrete building fronted by a parking lot with more bicycles than cars.

Kriminalassistent Mogens Hansen, a sandy-haired, pale man running to fat, greeted me terribly politely at the front desk where I had waited some ten minutes. His office was a small gray cell with prescription furniture. A couple of posters, possibly representing his own unfulfilled dreams, provided sunshine from the Mediterranean and snowscapes from the Alps. His desk had a computer and a black telephone.

He offered me a red plastic chair in Post-modern Danish, and I presented my credentials. Mogens Hansen listened politely to my story and occasionally wrote down a few words on a notepad. He wore one of the widest wedding bands I'd ever seen on anyone, proclaiming to all the world that here was a *married man*. When I stopped talking he contemplated his own written words for a long time before he addressed me.

"You are looking for a woman who has not been reported missing," he stated, and glanced at me briefly. "You believe she arrived in Copenhagen several months ago and may never have left. You base this assumption on a missing boarding pass stub. And you haven't been allowed to check the passenger list from Copenhagen to London because the airline is being uncooperative."

The way he presented it made me wonder what I was doing pursuing this flimsy lead in Denmark. But I was here and must persevere.

"I understand that the missing boarding pass stub could be a fluke," I admitted. "After all, how many of us haven't lost or discarded that small stub."

Mogens Hansen nodded as if he, too, was a frequent traveler.

"And I understand that the airline won't bend the rules for me," I continued quite untruthfully because, in fact, those rules had been bent for me by several airlines in recent memory.

"Yes, they have rules and regulations," he said dryly, and was I mistaken, or did he sneak an amused glance at me? "Maybe it's an area where I can be of some help."

"That would be super."

"It will take some time, of course."

"Of course."

"Why don't you call me back a week from today and, hopefully, I will have an answer for you."

A week? How could a simple task like this take a week? He answered my unspoken question.

"I must report this in order to get permission to request the information from the airline. And the request to the airline must then be made in writing."

"Of course," I said and, no doubt unpardonably, yawned as jet-lag caught up with me again.

He smiled the cutest smile.

"I'm sorry," he said, "I should have offered you a cup of coffee."

"That's all right. You'll have to excuse me, I'm still trying to get over the time difference between Denmark and the States."

He got up. "Well, call me then."

"I will," I said and departed after giving him the name of my hotel and the phone number. Not that I imagined he would call me before the week was up. I had a feeling that when people here said 'a week,' it meant exactly seven days.

I stopped by the front desk at the hotel hoping to find Ghita who'd helped me phone the police station. But I was informed she would not be on duty until the morning. Then, I'm embarrassed to say, I slept the rest of the afternoon until Birgit called me.

"Sorry I had to drag you to my mother's house yesterday. I told you, you wouldn't enjoy it."

"But you're wrong," I said. "It was a wonderful experience. I feel quite a part of the family." I'm not sure she believed me. "And *you* didn't look as if you hated the good food."

She changed the subject.

"Any luck with the police?"

"Some. But no results for another week. I'm planning to inquire at hotels where they might have stayed."

"Didn't you say the husband had a distant cousin here? Could they have stayed in a private home?"

Hadn't Louise Higginbotham said that Elizabeth loved quaint little hotels and didn't like staying with relatives?

"Not very likely," I said. "I'm planning to start with the smaller, exclusive hotels in the neighborhood. It's a long shot but I can't think of where else to start."

"I'll help you. My article is almost finished, actually before it's due. I'll be free by Wednesday morning. My press pass will help. We'll think of a likely story."

"Thanks, I could use some help."

"Ah, don't mention it. I'm becoming quite curious myself. I bet we can solve this together."

I sat down in the black leather sofa and flipped through my notebook. I hadn't written down any of the events in Barbados and now tried to remedy this omission. I outlined the essential facts, my conversations with Louise, our excursion to the plantation and my search of Hugh Mattson's desk. There had been nothing in purple ink except for the brief notation on the back on the airline ticket folder. What had it said? I hadn't paid attention.

I closed my eyes and pictured myself at the desk. I had stood with a book in my hand. The dust-jacket had been red, with black print under and above a weird line-drawing. Faces or bodies? Men and/or women? I had a fleeting image of the name of a bird. Or a name beginning with B? Would the author have been Mattson's Danish cousin? The cousin he'd described as 'some sort of a writer'?

At midnight I grabbed the phone book, made a list of hotels and arranged them according to an inner city map to avoid re-tracing my own steps.

CHAPTER 25

It turned out to be much less complicated than I'd feared. The next morning my half-baked story went over well with Ghita, at the reception. Since I know that telling people I am a private investigator sets off anxieties, if not fears, and prompts most people to clam up, I avoided that little detail. Ghita listened sympathetically to my tale of woe. How I'd lost touch with my dear English aunt and uncle who now lived in Barbados. How I'd heard they were in Copenhagen a few months ago and, how, if I could only find their address in Barbados, which should be in the hotel registry, I could get back in touch with them. I omitted to tell her I didn't know which hotel they'd stayed at.

"Well, that shouldn't be too difficult," said Ghita. "I could look it up and copy down their address for you. I don't think anyone could object to that."

"No, I don't see why anyone would. You couldn't by any chance start right away?"

"Why, certainly. As soon as I get through check-out time at eleven I'll have a few quiet hours until check-in at three."

"I appreciate it so much. I'll be out all morning but I'll be back around two."

I ate a hurried lunch at a pub on *Vesterbrogade* across from the *Tivoli Gardens* before setting out on my quest. The first hotel was located on a side street behind the *Politiken* newspaper house, the paper for which Birgit was writing her articles about Christiania. The reception area was teeming with guests and I sat down on a sofa from where I could keep an eye on the counter. I stayed there a good fifteen minutes before I got my chance.

The desk clerk was alone, leaning on the counter, contemplating traffic outside the window. He wore small oval steel-rimmed glasses. His light brown hair was parted in the middle and the resulting two little wings made it look as if the top of his head was about to take off. I presented my travel agent persona. He accepted my card and scanned it quickly.

"Ms. Prescott," he said. "How can I help you?"

He looked efficient so I plunged right in. The story rolled off my tongue easily enough and he remained very polite even as he glanced casually at his watch.

"It would be a pleasure to help you," he said when he'd heard me out, and I waited for the 'but.' "But you must understand that we can't give out that kind of information. It's a privacy issue."

I lowered my eyes, thinking. When I looked up he was watching me ironically.

"Is this really your aunt and uncle," he said, "or are you trying to pull a fast one?"

He laughed and I laughed with him, not too sincerely. Then I looked him steadily in the eye. In this business you have to think on your feet.

"You've seen through me," I said. "They are not my aunt and uncle. They are former clients of mine who've run off without paying their quite substantial bill to my travel agency. I hate for people to get away with that. And since I happened to be in Copenhagen I thought I'd try to track them down. Probably a silly idea and quite useless."

"Quite."

"You're in the travel business," I said. "You know how it is. Look, here's the number I'm staying at. If you change your mind and want to help me, I'll be there for another week."

He didn't commit to anything but he didn't refuse my card or my request, either. I doubted I would have the strength to go through this nine more times. Maybe I should scrap the first story and use the one about travel agency fraud which had just come to me.

I strolled slowly through narrow streets clogged by cars, delivery trucks, bicyclists, and pedestrians. Looking up, I took in the roof lines of the buildings with their green copper turrets, cupolas, and elaborate window trims, all from the 1600s. Below street level by several steps I counted six pubs—all in the span of a few short blocks—before I arrived at the next three hotels.

The travel agency story definitely worked because the receptionists accepted my card and promised to look up the information during quiet moments in their busy schedules. I made a point of mentioning I would be back the following day. This earned me some insincere smiles.

Continuing down the main shopping street, the *Strøget*, I arrived at the King's New Square. I sauntered down towards the *Nyhavn* canal with its many sailing and fishing boats. Houses with three-hundred year old sag were painted blue, green, brown, and ochre, and their hand-blown window panes glinted in the sunlight. The basement shops displayed all the items a sailor could possibly want to acquire from sou'westers and brandy flasks, to tattoos.

I found a table under a white market umbrella at a café in front of number 17. A pleasantly soused sea salt joined me and offered me beer and more delights if I'd follow him onboard. I paid for his beer but declined his invitation. He went on his wobbly way to join a blowsy blonde at a different table. Moments later, his luck having turned, they left together.

I walked back to the square and down a side street where I approached the fifth hotel on my list. When I saw the patrician building with its Rococo facade I regretted I hadn't known about this hotel when I made my reservations. The lobby had oriental carpets and deep leather furniture and was dimly lit by *fin-de-siecle* lamps. The receptionist, who turned out to be the owner of the hotel, Mr. Bruno Halvorsen, a man in his near seventies with a balding head and large brown eyes, listened intently to my story and shook his head in sympathy at the end of it.

"I wish sincerely to help you," he said. "But it seems very doubtful that they should have stayed precisely at my hotel."

Nevertheless, he brought out an enormous ledger and flipped the pages infuriatingly slowly, one by one, peering at me regretfully at the turn of each, until he came to the last one. He looked at me with mournful puppy-dog eyes.

"They did not stay with us," he said.

I cleared my throat and took out one of my PI cards and jotted down the name and phone number of my hotel. I watched him study the card and then he looked up with a puzzled expression on his pale face.

"There's something I need to explain," I said thinking I could use an ally familiar with hotels and with the city. "I'm sorry I didn't tell you the true story right away. I am actually investigating the possible disappearance of Mrs. Mattson."

"Oh, how terrible." Bruno Halvorsen's brown eyes had grown very large.

"I discovered that the Mattsons visited Denmark from London and I'm here looking for people who may have seen them. You see, it's possible that Mrs. Mattson did not return to England with her husband after all."

"It's like a detective story," said Halvorsen.

"It is, indeed. Do you have any suggestions of other hotels in the neighborhood that I could visit?"

"I will do better than that. I will personally telephone several places and see if I can get the information for you. That will save your shoe-leather." His eyes twinkled, he came around the counter, took my arm in a friendly grip, and escorted me to the door.

I looked at my watch. One-thirty. Time for a walk through the inner city visiting new and used bookstores.

CHAPTER 26

I walked back in the direction of the town hall square turning up and down side streets whenever I spotted the telltale wooden stands outside bookstores.

It soon became clear that looking for a book with a red cover was like looking for that elusive needle. Inside the little shops the books did appear in alphabetical order on shelves but it soon became equally clear that there weren't many Danish authors whose last names began with B.

The streets were crowded with people, most hurrying home with paper totes, but many walking leisurely, browsing with me in the book stands. Young women with backpacks vacillating before the many possibilities, and young men following them about. Older guys with scraggly beards and torn jeans contemplated the cheap offerings. One particularly malodorous man stayed at my side until I had to remove myself. No one ever seemed to buy any books.

It was with relief that I came upon a large bookstore selling new books. Inside, the atmosphere was hushed much like at a library with people speaking in whispers or not at all. Silent browsing was the by-word and I soon stood in front of the Bs of Danish literature.

There was Bendix, Bjornvig, Blicher, Blixen, Bodelsen, Bonnevie and Brogger but nothing which sounded remotely like Bird and nothing at all with a red dust jacket. Consulting with the salesperson I found it hard to explain what exactly I was looking for and he soon gave up on me.

I continued in this fashion for another half an hour occasionally meeting up with the same group of students and, to my dismay, even the smelly individual from whom I distanced myself again.

Almost back at my hotel I made one last effort and entered another large bookstore. Having quickly run out of authors with names beginning with B, I proceeded to chase down all red dust jackets on the shelves. I pulled them out one by one but none looked even close to the one I remembered.

I gave up for the day and decided to catch Lillian at her antique store instead. I picked up my rental car from the parking lot near the hotel and set out in a northerly direction towards *Nørrebrogade*. Imposing old apartment buildings, probably built in the mid-1800s, lined the first part of the wide street. But on the other side of a bridge they gave way to different kinds of buildings without balconies or ornamentation, with narrow windows and doors. I felt I had now left the more prosperous city and was entering an area not pictured in my glossy guidebook.

Lillian's shop was located half way down the street and I watched the numbers as I rode along. I found parking without much difficulty and looked around in amazement. Was this Denmark? Dark-complexioned women, their heads under complicated scarves. Men with heavy mustaches and bold eyes watching their sidewalk vegetable stands. The air filled with the sounds of guttural language. Now and then blonde women with pert noses wandering in and out of shops followed by dark men's eyes.

A bell clanged loudly when I opened the door to the antique shop. The grimy window said *'gamle møbler'* which I took to mean old furniture, but a small sign swinging on a chain above the door proclaimed *'antikviteter.'* I stepped carefully inside the musty-smelling shop and the bell clanged again when I closed the door. A bundle of clothing behind a glass counter moved and revealed a wrinkled face with rheumy eyes.

"I'm looking for Lillian," I said tentatively.

I was afraid that the assertion 'English spoken here' would once again prove false but this time I was wrong. The bundle heaved, a person emerged and before me stood a frail figure who answered me in the Queen's English.

"She should be back momentarily," he pronounced succinctly. "She is concluding some business next door. Won't you please sit down and wait. Or," he added, when I hesitated, mainly because I didn't see where I could possibly sit, "maybe you prefer to browse. My name is Fredrik."

"Thank you, Fredrik," I said. "I think I'd like to browse."

"There are more rooms at the back." He pointed a thin arm. "Feel free. Quite a number of interesting books."

I couldn't help wondering what had brought an educated gentleman to descend into squalor, dressed in wrinkled clothes, liberally spotted, obviously ill-nourished with translucent skin, lanky hair, and several missing teeth.

Fredrik sat down looking as if our conversation had drained him of what little energy he'd had when I entered. I wended my way around haphazard piles of china, magazines, books, lamp bases, picture frames, and enameled kitchen ware leaning against the legs of old furniture. Behind glass and lock, in several cupboards, I spotted silverware and porcelain sitting on antique embroidered linen.

In the back room books were stacked on shelves in alphabetical order according to subject. There were even three sections with English, French, and German books. I looked at the English mysteries, since these are what I read when I travel. I randomly picked out a couple of hard covers and turned around at the sound of Lillian's voice.

"Hello, there," she said. "So nice of you to drop by. Fredrik will be pleased that you're looking at his books. I call them "his" because he decides what we buy."

"All very well organized," I said. "Was he a librarian?"

"No, no, he taught English in high school for many years." Lillian looked towards the door and whispered. "He ran into some trouble with young girls and lost his position. A long time ago. He has worked here more than ten years. Although you might not think so, he's very dependable and I can leave the shop in his care."

The only trouble, I thought, might be that he didn't follow anyone around but just sat there half asleep. I turned back to the bookshelf and half-heartedly looked at Danish novels. There was nothing at all under B and nothing with a red cover. Until the very last shelf.

I pulled it out.

I stared at the crude line drawing and tried to determine whether the book should be classified as science-fiction or pornography. There was no doubt in my mind. This was the book I was looking for, the book I'd seen on Hugh Mattson's desk. The author was one Ambrosius Vogel.

Vogel, I thought. What happened to B? And, uninvited, my early German lessons popped up in my mind and brought me an image of Vogel equaling Bird. I mentally hung my head. Bob Makowski wouldn't have thanked me for this one.

Lillian took one look at the cover and laughed.

"You must ask Fredrik," she said. "The author is a friend of his, that's probably why we have his books. I don't know what they're about but I can guess. Are you sure you want it?"

I nodded, kept the book in my hand, and followed Lillian to the front where Fredrik was assisting a customer. I paid for the book and for a silver-plated serving tray I didn't really need and the next thing I knew, Fredrik had left and Lillian was getting ready to close shop.

"Oh, no," I said. "I wanted to ask him about the author of this book. When will he be back?"

"Tomorrow. If he has a good day he'll be here by ten."

I stood on the sidewalk, undecided. On this street I saw no pleasant outdoor cafés, no tourists strolling along leisurely. Instead, working class people went about their business with worried faces. Men huddled in doorways, half-smoked cigarettes dangling at the corner of their lips, empty beer bottles on the stoop next to feet in worn shoes.

On my way to the car I stopped at a traffic light and, while I waited, my eyes fell on a corner pub. Through the window I saw the withered frame of Fredrik, his head bent pensively over a glass of beer. I turned in my tracks and in two seconds flat stood inside the door to the café where stale air surrounded me like an old blanket. Fredrik didn't look up until I sat down opposite him at the table.

It would be an exaggeration to say that his rheumy eyes lit up, but near enough. His faded pink cardigan was buttoned crookedly across his sunken chest.

"Jamie Prescott," I said, but even if he'd offered me his hand I couldn't have taken it. It was covered with eczema of a particularly red and scaly variety. "We just met at Lillian's antique shop."

A drop of water sat at the tip of his nose, wavered, and fell on the scarf he had wound several times around his neck. He looked into his beer glass and nodded.

"I was interested in the books you have acquired for the store. You have organized everything admirably. I thought you might have been a librarian, you certainly know your stuff."

When he still nodded without verbalizing an answer I had to plod on.

"In particular, I noticed a book by an author named Ambrosius Vogel. Lillian says that he's a friend of yours. I wonder if you can tell me where I can find him. I've bought his book and would like him to autograph it for me."

Now he looked up.

"A nice lady like you," he said. "You wouldn't want to read a book like that. And you wouldn't want to meet the author, either."

Startled, and not a little anxious about the way this was shaping up, I back-tracked.

"It's not really for me since I don't read Danish but I have some disreputable friends here who'd enjoy the book."

"*I* don't even enjoy his books." Fredrik drank deeply from his beer mug and wiped his nose on a threadbare sleeve. "He's a pervert."

"Oh, come now, there must be something to his writing if it's been published."

"Some people will publish anything. A nice lady like you shouldn't be involved," he repeated.

I'm not a lady, I wanted to reply, I'm a private investigator, and not that nice either, especially when I'm working on a case. I took a closer look at Fredrik trying to discern the personality behind the dilapidated shell. I made a quick decision.

"Fredrik."

"Mmm."

"I need your help. I don't really want his book but I must talk to Ambrosius Vogel. You're the only person who can give me his address. It is very important."

Fredrik took another swig of beer. He didn't answer me and I couldn't tell if my urgent voice had reached him. I hoped he wouldn't inquire into the nature of the urgency. But he only looked up expectantly when the waiter came by our table.

"Fredrik," I said. "I'm going to order some pasta and a salad and more beer. Will you join me?"

"Could we make it a hamburger and fries?"

"Sure thing."

When the food came, he threw himself at the plate. He chewed awkwardly with just his front teeth and, as a last gesture, cleaned the ketchup off his plate with a piece of bread. This might be the first full meal he'd had in a long time. Sadly, the way to his heart was probably through his stomach.

"Fredrik. Let's have dessert and coffee," I said and signed to the waiter who brought over two portions of rice pudding with a fierce red cherry sauce. The coffee was the black kind which set my hair on end.

We ate in silence. After Fredrik had scraped his plate clean and consumed half his coffee, he leaned back against the wall and fumbled in his breast pocket for cigarettes. He inhaled deeply with half-closed eyes and blew the smoke past my left ear. I flinched but there was nowhere for me to go.

"His name is not Ambrosius Vogel at all. It's a fancy pseudonym he invented as a joke. Made him sound literary, he said, but what he writes is far from literature."

Fredrik suddenly opened his eyes as wide as his drooping lids allowed, and cackled.

"It isn't Shakespeare." The cackle turned into a cough which wouldn't stop. He closed his eyes and sat for so long that I feared the good food had put him to sleep before my mission was accomplished. I was just about to nudge him when he spoke without opening his eyes.

"His real name is just plain Anton Christensen. But I haven't seen him in several years and I don't know where he lives."

Fredrik watched me write down the name.

"Thank you very much, Fredrik." I folded the note and tucked it into my pocket. "I've got to run now. Maybe you'd like some more dessert and coffee?"

He nodded, and when the waiter brought him the second helping I got up from the table and left him eating not quite as greedily as the first time around.

Back at the hotel Ghita, the receptionist, greeted me with the sad news that she'd been unable to trace the Mattsons. I must have been mistaken about the hotel they'd stayed at, she said, and I had to agree.

The phone book didn't offer up a listing for an Ambrosius Vogel. There were people with such fanciful variations as Vogelgesang and Vogelmutter, with initials G. and H. and Z. There was only one Vogel, and his first name was Valdemar, no way near Ambrosius. And there were fifty columns of Christensen but no one with the first name of Anton. For the sake of thoroughness, I called information to see if the names were unlisted. The answer was negative. Neither Ambrosius nor Anton seemed to exist.

Surprisingly, Kriminalassistent Mogens Hansen had left a message for me to call him immediately. It would have to wait until the morning.

CHAPTER 27

"Elizabeth Mattson did not leave Copenhagen on the same flight as her husband. Her ticket is still open."

My heartbeat increased slowly until I felt a burning sensation in my throat and a stricture in my chest. I closed my eyes, took a couple of deep breaths. What I feared had come true. Elizabeth had never returned to England.

"Hello?" said Kriminalassistent Mogens Hansen. "Are you there?"

"Sir, I am so sorry, yes, I'm here. I am just speechless at your news. Even if it's something I was afraid had happened, I'm stunned. And I hadn't expected for you to have any results until the end of the week. Thank you so much."

"Of course, just because she didn't leave by air doesn't mean she didn't leave Denmark. One can go from here to England by any number of other routes. There are trains from Copenhagen down through Europe to several ports with connections to England. Or even through the tunnel from France straight into London. She could have quarreled with her husband and gone her separate way."

"Yes, of course, there's always that possibility. She could have returned to England on her own, and she could have died there just as her husband claims."

Then I told him about Bob Makowski's search in England for the alleged place of death to determine if the death certificate was a fake.

"Admirable," he said. "In the meantime, though, what will you do? From our point of view, at the official level, there is nothing for us to pursue as yet. But, unofficially, I assure you of my sincere wish to help."

"I am most appreciative. The owner of the *Crown Hotel* in Bredgade is calling his colleagues at other hotels in the neighborhood to find out where the Mattsons might have stayed, but I'm afraid it's a long shot."

"Unfortunately, tracing travelers in Europe has now become very difficult. No one is required to report where they plan to stay or if they're on legitimate business. But I'll make some inquiries. Unofficially, of course."

"Of course. There is just one more thing you could do for me right now."

"If at all possible."

"Because of my unfortunate lack of knowledge of your language and, although everyone speaks such good English, every inquiry takes me forever. I want to locate an Anton Christensen who writes under the pseudonym of Ambrosius Vogel. I've already established that he is not in the phone book under either name, nor does he have an unlisted phone."

"And who is he?"

"I believe he may be a cousin of Hugh Mattson's. He may have nothing whatsoever to do with Elizabeth Mattson's disappearance but I want to find him even if it turns out to be a blind alley."

"And do you know the name of the publisher of his book?"

I pulled out the book and spelled out the name of the publisher.

"That should help to locate the right Anton Christensen. I'll call you back. It won't take me long."

"Now that *is* good news," I said, and he laughed. "I'll wait by the phone until I hear from you. And thank you so much, I really appreciate your help."

I paced in front of the window debating my next move. I decided against calling Louise with the news that Mogens Hansen had just brought me. I didn't want that information to spread like wildfire across the isle of Barbados. Instead I called Bob Makowski and got him on the line just as he arrived at his office.

"Hey," he shouted, "what's new in Copenhagen?"

"I've enlisted the help of a most accommodating criminal investigator at the police station who has just informed me that Elizabeth indeed did not leave Copenhagen with her husband, at least not by air."

I explained Mogens Hansen's theory that Elizabeth could have returned to England separately from her husband by a combination of train and boat.

"The missing boarding pass stub was no fluke after all," I said.

"I told you I had a feeling about this."

"So you did. What I need now is to find out if the death certificate is fake. Then this will be a missing person's case as far as the police are concerned and Hugh Mattson is in deep trouble. Have you heard from your guy in England?"

"Not yet, why don't I give him a holler and get his ass moving. I'll get back to you."

The minute I hung up with Bob, Mogens Hansen came on the line sounding quite self-satisfied.

"I told you it wouldn't take long," he said. "Write down this address."

He spelled it out for me and I wrote it down laboriously not even trying to pronounce the name of the street.

"It's one of the side streets just beyond the main train station. Not a very comfortable part of town but you'll be all right there during the day. Good luck."

The dismal side streets to *Vesterbrogade* in the Western part of the city turned out to be mirror images of the ones I'd just left in the Northern part. Pawnshops and tobacconists, porn shops and greengroceries, competed for space in the red brick buildings. Anton Christensen, a.k.a. Ambrosius Vogel, lived on the sixth floor according to the list of names inside the door of number 10. The small entrance with its cracked tiled floor was grimy and foul-smelling with empty beer bottles and stained newspapers heaped in one corner. Climbing the stairs I refrained from touching the handrail.

His name was on the door and I rang the bell. And rang again. A shadow moved across a small spy hole, a chain rattled, and the door was opened just enough to admit an eye looking at me.

"Hello," I said and, through the crack, offered him my card—the one with just my name and address. "My name is Jamie Prescott, I was sent here by Fredrik, I'm interested in your latest book."

The chain rattled, and the door swung open. Before me stood a disgusting man. Hanging belly, grubby shorts and undershirt, stubbly gray beard, rheumy eyes á lá Fredrik, greasy hair, and beer breath. I took an involuntary step back.

"You a publisher?" He looked me up and down before he stood aside to let me in.

"You a publisher?" he repeated.

"Not exactly." I stepped into the narrow hallway. A door to the right led into a dreary looking kitchen. Two other doors stood wide open, one to a disorderly living room, the other to a bedroom with an unmade bed. Unexpectedly, the blanket heaved and a head of unwashed hair appeared above it. A pair of startled blue eyes looked at me from a child's face. He's a pedophile, I thought, in shock. The girl looked no more than twelve. Was this where poor Fredrik had met his Waterloo ten years ago?

I will deal with this in a minute, I thought, and turned to Anton Christensen. We were still in the narrow corridor and

I had no great desire to proceed into the living area but did, since this was what I had come for.

I sat down on the edge of a chair piled high with newspapers and got on with business.

"Do you understand my English?"

"Of course."

"I've just come from Barbados where I met with your cousin, Hugh Mattson."

"I do not have a cousin in Barbados."

"But you do know someone by the name of Hugh Mattson?"

Anton Christensen shook his head doubtfully and I suddenly felt my self-confidence wane.

"I spoke to Hugh Mattson in Barbados just a few weeks ago. He had your book on his desk and said his cousin in Denmark was 'some kind of a writer.' That description seems to fit you."

"Who are you?" he said and scratched his belly. "I thought Fredrik sent you. Aren't you a book buyer?"

"I'm a private investigator looking into the disappearance of Hugh Mattson's wife, Elizabeth," I said, and watched the expression on Anton Christensen's face. A mixture of fear and cunning. I decided to exploit the fear.

"If you have any information at all I would advise you to speak up," I said. "The police are now investigating."

"Why are you here, then, and not the police?"

"Because I'm one step ahead of them and if you're smart you'll tell me what you know."

"This has nothing to do with my books?"

"No. Did you see the Mattsons in Copenhagen about three months ago?"

"I want you to leave," he said.

I looked towards the bedroom where I heard someone moving about, opening and closing drawers. Anton Christensen watched me furtively.

"She's way underage," I said. "There must be laws against this."

"She's 18," he said, just as the twelve-year old appeared in the doorway to the living room. She was taller than I'd expected and she looked at me with a knowing and insolent expression.

"*Hasta la vista, baby,*" she said to Anton. She didn't favor me with a goodbye. I sighed.

I scribbled the phone number at the hotel on the back of another card and gave it to him.

"Call me when you unlock your lips," I said. "And it had better be soon."

Scum, I fumed to myself, as I took the steps down two at a time to escape from the dirty surroundings. When I got to the street I saw the girl hanging out with a group of what looked like classmates. Twelve years old if a day. They all carried school bags, only she did not. I decided to let Mogens Hansen know about her. Surely, somewhere, parents or teachers should be informed.

I had left my rental car in the parking lot near the hotel and had come by taxi. I was walking towards *Vesterbrogade* when I became aware of the clop-clop of wooden clogs on the sidewalk. I turned my head automatically but the only person behind me was a man dressed in working clothes with a tool box slung over his shoulder. He had a round fat face under a blue cap and wore black clogs. The next time I looked around he was disappearing into a doorway. Take it easy, I said to myself, don't go all paranoid at this point. But old habits will prevail.

When I tried to hail a taxi to return to the hotel they all sailed past me without stopping. It was rush hour and instead of wasting my time on the curb with my arm in the air I joined the pedestrian stream. I crossed the widening street in front of the train station and stopped at the *Royal Hotel* to gaze at the displays of glass and jewelry in its windows. I should probably get my mother and Topsy a souvenir from here. But not today.

At the hotel, Ghita greeted me as a long-lost friend and commiserated with me about my lost relatives, the Mattsons. Apart from my investigative deviousness, I'm essentially a truthful person and Ghita's naive friendliness made me uncomfortable. As a result, I spent several minutes in amiable conversation trying to compensate for my guilty feelings before taking the elevator upstairs.

I called Mogens Hansen and caught him just as he was leaving the station. I told him about the girl in Anton Christensen's apartment. Mogens Hansen sounded disgusted, as I knew he would, and I had a pretty good feeling that he would take some appropriate action.

"I have another bit of unofficial news for you," he said. "I'm running a check on reports from hospitals and morgues for any Jane Doe brought in during the last six months. No luck so far but I'm not through yet. I'll call you tomorrow."

Mogens Hansen's enthusiasm and initiative cheered me to such a degree that I decided to take a solitary swing through the *Tivoli Gardens*. Dusk had fallen and the entrance—a romanticized Arc d'Triomphe—was outlined in rainbow-colored bulbs. I stood in line to pay the equivalent of five dollars and went through the turnstile.

I stopped at the pantomime theater where Pierrot in white, Columbine in a tutu, and Harlequin in black, green and white checkered tights, played out a *Commedia dell'arte* classic. The applause drifted up in the early evening air and I felt Pierrot, with his enormous red lips and stark black eyebrows, look directly at me.

I sat down in a café where I had a cup of that black Danish coffee that could raise the dead. Not a bad day, all told, I thought. And then I was superstitious enough to regret feeling smug and quickly thought about something rotten in the State of Denmark.

CHAPTER 28

Bruno Halvorsen called me at seven in the morning and I was immediately wide awake.

"Good news, good news!" His voice crackled with emotion. "I've found your missing persons. They stayed at a hotel further up my street and I'll take you there at ten o'clock to speak to the receptionist who remembers taking care of them."

My heart took a turn around the block and almost stopped. I was about to hit the jackpot. I was raring to do something—anything—and to go somewhere—anywhere. But, instead, since it was now only seven-fifteen I got rid of my pent-up energy by doing a hundred push-ups followed by an excess of jumping jacks.

I had just showered and dressed and left a message for Mogens Hansen when the phone rang again.

"Gooooood morninnnng," a voice came across sounding like Robin Williams in Vietnam. "Rise and shine. I'm in the lobby. Can I come up?"

Birgit, my second or third cousin twice or more removed. She looked around the room and apparently approved of what she saw. She had left the muumuu behind and today was dressed in something flowing to her ankles that looked like a skirt but might be pants and, on top of this, an equally loose-flowing blouse. She had remained faithful to her Birkenstocks.

"Very nice. What, you haven't had breakfast yet? We'll soon fix that," she chirped and called room service. She mumbled and laughed, laughed and mumbled, with the result that a tray for two was soon delivered to my room. Omelette, cheese, Danish pastry, croissants, real butter, fattening cream—what else—and coffee. Enough to feed an army.

I ate and drank sparingly while Birgit wolfed down the rest. Her flowing garments would hide the result. My skin-tight jeans would not.

"Hans left for India this morning," she said.

"And you're happy?"

"Oh, no. Yes. Maybe." She laughed and looked only slightly embarrassed.

"Don't apologize," I said. "It's all right to want some time to yourself. How long will he be gone?"

"I don't know," she said and looked as if she meant 'I don't care'.

That was rather surprising given the affectionate clutches I'd seen them in.

"It's not as if he contributes to the rent on the apartment," she said. "So, from that point of view, it doesn't matter how long he's gone. The main thing right now is that I've finished my Christiania articles and am about to start the next series. But today I'm all yours, ready to help find your missing person. And, later, I've got this terrific guy, a photographer, who wants to meet you."

I let this information sink in and wondered briefly if she was planning a double date. I thought of all the mismatches Topsy has dreamed up for me over the years. She cannot bear my state of being single at forty-two. For reasons known only to herself Topsy favors no type in particular for me as long as he's unattached—or maybe only in the process of becoming unattached. And heaven knew what Birgit's take on me would turn out to be. Time would tell.

Bruno Halvorsen was waiting on the doorstep to his hotel wiping his hands on a bright red handkerchief. A bow-tie, a striped shirt, and a tweed jacket, made him look like a distracted Oxford professor. I introduced him to Birgit but it was my arm he took solicitously to shepherd me across the street. I let him do it although that kind of chivalry counts high on my list of least favored moves. We went past patrician houses and pricey antique shops, past the Marble Church with its circular green cupola presiding across from the Queen's palace, and arrived at a small hotel tucked away in a side street. Vilhelm, the receptionist, remembered the Mattsons clearly.

"I believe they were actually British, at least that's the way they spoke." He screwed up his face, thinking. "My wife and I have always talked about vacationing in Barbados, that's one reason I recall them."

"How did they seem?" I said, not quite knowing the answer I was looking for.

"Seem? Well, now that you ask, they seemed to be arguing whenever I saw them. We serve breakfast at the hotel from 7 to 10 in the morning and I noticed that either they didn't speak at all, or else they were quite loud, especially he."

"What did they argue about?"

"I don't know, I didn't hear the words, only loud voices. I worried it would bother the other guests."

"Do you have any idea what they did while they were here?"

"I imagine they did what tourists do. Maybe they took some escorted bus tours. No, no, wait, they rented a car. He complained about the parking problem. That seems to be all I remember," Vilhelm said.

I couldn't think of anything else except maybe circling around the same territory one more time in the hopes of ferreting out another tidbit of information. And that's what I did. I made Vilhelm tell me the story again. He was able to add only one more thing.

"On Sunday, Mrs. Mattson asked me where she could find a church and I directed her to the English church close to the *Langelinie* harbor near the *Gefion* fountain."

"And did she go?"

"I believe so. She asked if the church was within walking distance and I told her it was."

"How long did they stay with you?"

"About a week or so. What I do recall is that they departed late one afternoon and had to pay for an extra night, and I remember he didn't protest. Some guests become unpleasant and think they should be able to overstay for free."

"Did he say why they were leaving?"

"He said his wife wasn't feeling well, in fact, he said she was waiting outside in the car and that he had come back by himself to get their suitcases and to check out. He said they were on their way to the airport."

"You mean you didn't see her before they left?"

"I saw her in the morning before they went out. No, wait a minute, I am just thinking. I don't believe I saw her that very morning. Somehow, I remember saying to myself how peaceful it was at breakfast with only him there. No arguing going on."

That meant Elizabeth Mattson had not been seen—at least not at the hotel—since the day before Hugh left Denmark.

I thanked Bruno Halvorsen with many 'tusind tak' which I was now throwing about as my only Danish phrase. He went back to his hotel and Birgit and I picked up my car.

"Come along," I said. "We're going to the English church."

"You want to go to church on a week-day?" Birgit's expression indicated that she was ready to accept my peculiar American behavior.

"No, I want to see if the vicar is in and if he, by any chance, remembers Elizabeth Mattson."

"How will that help you? Would she have gone to confession? And even if she did, isn't that confidential?"

"As far as I know, the Anglican church does not offer confession. She just might have spoken to him informally."

The church probably should not have been open on a week-day morning, but it was. A young guy in jeans and a green sweater stood on the steps squinting in the sunlight, perfectly framed by the gothic archway. He beamed at us as we walked across the cobblestones leading to the steps.

"Hi," I said.

"How do you do. Are you British?"

"No, American. I'm looking for the vicar."

"Well, you've found him. I'm Ian Thompson. What can I do for you? If you need a respite from your busy life as tourists, you've come to the right place."

Unexpectedly unconventional, I thought. He took us inside his small church, almost as small as Elizabeth Mattson's chapel in Barbados. Beyond the first ten rows on either side of the aisle there were three rows of pews perpendicular to the altar. It was in one of these that the vicar invited us to sit. I gave him my story, quite simplified, about Barbados, and about searching for Elizabeth, and while I spoke he looked more and more concerned.

"I am here," I concluded, "to follow a lead from the receptionist at the hotel where she was staying. He said that Mrs. Mattson intended to go to your church. This would have been the second Sunday in May. I am almost feeling silly suggesting that you would remember a stray congregant from so long ago. You probably have tourists drop in at services all the time."

"No," Reverend Thompson said with a wry smile. "We have a small faithful core of British worshipers but I can't in all honesty say that the church is full every Sunday. At Christmas and Easter, yes, of course."

"So, it would be unusual for an outsider to show up for services?"

"Unhappily, yes. But in this case, rather fortunate. You see, I remember Mrs. Mattson very well indeed. She was a troubled soul. When the congregants left the church she hung back while I stood at the door and shook hands. I could tell immediately that she needed someone to talk to. I invited her back inside and we sat down where you and I are sitting right now."

I shifted in my seat and thought of the other occasion when I had sat in a pew previously occupied by Elizabeth.

"She was carrying a small leather-bound bible. I asked her if she would like a cup of tea, but she refused. Gradually, she told me all about it. She had left a troublesome daughter behind in Barbados. It seems the daughter was involved with drugs and very unsavory friends. Her husband, I gathered, had been unfaithful to her for years and, it seemed, was somewhat abusive. She had been on the verge of seeking a divorce before their trip to England but had agreed, at her husband's pleading, to give him and the marriage one more chance."

"Did she say what brought them to Denmark?"

"No, only that her husband had suggested a vacation here. At any rate, it seemed to me that just being able to talk to someone about her problems made her feel better."

"And what advice did you give her?" Birgit said looking like someone who never asked for advice.

"Well, being a married man myself, although not of such long standing, I assured her that many a problem can be solved with good will on both sides. It seemed that her husband was sincere in wanting to make up for past mistakes.

He wanted her to have a pleasant vacation and to rent a boat for a week to take her sailing up the coast of Zealand. I must say I found that a very pleasant prospect, but apparently Mrs. Mattson did not. It seemed that sailing was his consuming interest in life and that she had never been able to share it. I told her I felt she must accompany her husband if that is what it would take to mend things between them."

"You told her that?" I said, and I'm afraid my voice and my facial expression betrayed me. Across the seas from Barbados I could hear the voice of Louise Higginbotham:

"*Elizabeth is deathly afraid of the water, never learned to swim, never goes sailing with Hugh.*"

"You don't agree with my advice?"

"Under normal circumstances it might have been quite good advice. But I'm afraid neither you nor I know what kind of a person her husband is or what he might be capable of."

Ian Thompson looked stricken. We exchanged cards with phone numbers and e-mail addresses after which Birgit and I said our good-byes.

"We're going up the coast to find the marina where Hugh Mattson rented a boat," I said.

Fifteen minutes later we cruised up the *Strandvejen* towards Elsinore. On our right the coast of Sweden was clearly visible across the blue waters of the *Øresund*.

CHAPTER 29

The water was calm as a mirror with only an occasional small wave breaking gently and immediately disappearing. A string of boats, their white sails slack, dotted the water. On our left, large white Italianate villas stood surrounded by immaculate hedges. The two lane road wound through small villages with thatched farm houses painted white or, surprisingly, deep pink. A white apartment building—sleek as a luxury liner—floated high up on a hill, window panes glittering in the sunlight.

The marinas appeared seemingly within a few feet of one another along the coast. The routine felt all too familiar to me having gone through it at the hotels in the inner city of Copenhagen. With Birgit staying in the background I presented myself pretending to look for my long-lost relatives, the Mattsons. Some of the marinas had no offices at all, the business of sailing being conducted without bureaucracy. At others, polite young women and men in appropriate sailing attire, disclaimed any knowledge of rentals of sailboats. By the seventh rejection I began to lose hope.

"I don't know anything about sailing," Birgit said, revealing herself to be an unusual Dane. "But it does seem strange that no one has found renting a lucrative business. Let's push on."

Which is what we did until hunger led us to a larger than usual marina halfway up the coast to Elsinore. I parked the car in a fairly big lot and we walked across a path of ominously crunching flintstone shards towards a small restaurant. It was housed in an unpretentious wooden building stained dark brown. The dining room faced the marina where sailboats glided along a narrow canal and disappeared towards the open sea.

The waitress—a very young woman acting like a student performing a social experiment—explained the specialties of the day. My preference for the à là carte menu brought her to the edge of confusion. The food arrived after a half hour interval during which she conferred frantically with another youngster who may or may not have been the cook.

When we dawdled over coffee I suddenly realized that Birgit had not lit up any of her interminable cigarettes the entire morning.

"Don't tell me you've quit smoking?"

"Aha, you finally noticed?" Birgit pulled up her left sleeve and showed me the patch. "I'm starting a new life in more ways than one. Actually, it was more like my doctor who decided for me. Said I'm getting asthma. Like my mother."

"Well, whatever the reason, I congratulate you." I could now imagine having Birgit as a house-guest in Bethesda.

After lunch we strolled towards a row of small shops in A-frame houses facing the water. Rust-colored boulders secured the coastline and narrow boardwalks led to several dozen sailboats at anchor. Most had the Danish flag hoisted high, the white cross on a red background fluttering in the air. Coils of yellow cord were neatly attached to wooden posts.

A few people in white sailor pants—a color which always strikes me as particularly unsuited to the proximity of oil and grease—sat at outdoor cafés licking philosophically at large cones of ice-cream.

The last shop was a sales center for sail- and speedboats. They had a small model in the window of a Nauticat 321 surrounded by seashells and white sand plus a sign which Birgit told me meant 'See Sales Personnel Within.' Not a word about rentals. Birgit and I looked at one another in despair. Even though the youngsters at the last marina had said that rentals might be available at bigger places further north, they had struck me as being strangely uninformed.

We entered the shop and stood around a good while listening to a voice in the back. I had picked up several brochures about boats for sale, about mooringlines and trimlines and paints, when I decided to move towards the voice. I found it coming from a suntanned guy leaning back leisurely in his chair, speaking into a phone. He waved to me casually, mouthed the inevitable *lige et øjeblik*, and continued talking. I returned to Birgit with the good news that a live person would soon be attending us.

As good as my word he came out looking lively—a bit older than at first glance—which made Birgit perk up noticeably.

"Do you rent out boats?" I asked bluntly.

"You mean do we have charter boats?" he said in perfect English.

"Yes, I guess that's what I mean. Charter." I said. Somehow, I associated "charter" with large-scale operations involving hundreds of travelers.

"Yes, certainly. Wait just a sec," he said, and went back to his office. He returned and handed me several price lists headed 'Charter Boats by The Week.' I studied them in silence with Birgit peeking over my shoulder. There were four types of sailboats ranging in price from the equivalent of fifteen hundred to two thousand dollars per week. Since I wasn't going to rent a boat—no less charter one—I used our few moments of silence to prepare my next move.

Patience having worn thin, I plunged right in. I handed him my private investigator card.

His suntan became a tad more rosy as he must have scanned his memory for any problem which would require the attention of a private investigator.

"Miss Prescott, my name is Anders," he said.

I quickly went through my little speech about the Mattsons. I threw in a few words about Kriminalassistent Mogens Hansen in Copenhagen and embellished upon former speeches by saying that I knew a Hugh Mattson from Barbados had "chartered" a boat somewhere in this vicinity during the month of May.

"Could you verify whether he chartered one from you?" I concluded, having left out the reason I needed to know. Anders bowed immediately to perceived authority.

"I'll get the lists," he said. "The way it works, the charter week starts on a Saturday at four in the afternoon and ends the following Saturday at ten in the morning."

If Elizabeth had been to church on a Sunday and Hugh Mattson had left Denmark the following Wednesday, Monday or Tuesday must be when it happened, if anything had happened at all. The window of opportunity was that small.

"Do people sometimes charter a boat during the middle of the week?"

"And pay for the whole week if they only go out a couple of days?" He looked incredulous. "Not that I can ever recall. But I am not here all the time, I have a partner whom I could call."

"Let's first see if you can find Mattson's name."

I followed Anders back to his office, with Birgit in tow. She struck up an animated conversation with him in Danish and I could tell that Hans would soon be good riddance in India.

As had countless receptionists in Copenhagen—at small hotels which had not yet entered the age of computerized reservations—Anders brought out a ledger. He opened it to a page which said 'Maj.'

"Here he is," Anders said. Then he looked closer at the handwriting and said. "Oh, no, I thought that was the name but now I see it says 'Hugo Madsen.' That's a Danish name and I thought you said he's from Barbados. Could it be the same person?"

"I don't know." My head started to spin. "I imagine you have some sort of registration form people fill out. Can you lay your hands on this one?"

Anders jumped to it and soon produced the form.

"What do you require in the way of identification?" I said.

"Identification? Nothing. The full amount is paid in advance by bank check or credit card. The insurance is included in the price and you pay for your own gas."

"So, you don't ask people for their driver's licenses or, in the case of foreigners, their passports?"

"No, they just write their address on the form." Anders pointed. "Look, he lives in Copenhagen. Although I see he didn't put down his phone number. And he paid in cash. How unusual."

I looked at the form. Hugh Mattson, a.k.a. Hugo Madsen had entered the address of his literary cousin, Anton Christensen, a.k.a. Ambrosius Vogel. No mention of Barbados.

He's not British. He's Danish, I thought.

If it was true that he had arrived in Barbados on a boat from England when had he left Denmark? Had he lived in England long enough to become a naturalized citizen? Why had he suppressed his Danish background. Or had he? Hadn't he simply said he had a Danish cousin on his mother's side? Did that mean that his mother had married in England and that he was, indeed, British? Then why use the Danish spelling 'Hugo Madsen?'

"When did he charter the boat," I asked.

"On a Tuesday. He lost three whole days," Anders said disapprovingly. "He chartered the least expensive boat."

"When did he return it?"

"Probably the following Saturday morning." Anders looked closer at the ledger and then at me. "That's funny. My partner noted down here that although the customer had said he needed the boat for what remained of the week, he had delivered it back on Wednesday or thereabouts."

"Thereabouts?"

"Yes, my partner—according to his notation—found the boat Wednesday morning, moored in good order but without an explanation. Could even have come in late Tuesday night."

And Hugh Mattson had left Denmark Wednesday afternoon. I could feel my stomach turn.

"Could you possibly let me have a photocopy of the page in your ledger and of the registration form?" I endeavored to look official. "Kriminalassistent Mogens Hansen may wish to see them."

I had no need to apologize for an unusual request. Anders was at the copier in a flash, no doubt eager to be rid of me but, who knew. Danes seemed disarmingly innocent and trusting. When I stuffed the copies in my bag I saw Birgit hand Anders her card.

An enterprising woman.

CHAPTER 30

I still couldn't believe what I'd just discovered. I borrowed Birgit's cell phone. For once Mogens Hansen was out so I left a message. He would have to check if a Hugo Madsen had a criminal record and had left Denmark under a cloud.

On our way back to town I tried to visualize Elizabeth Farley Granger Mattson's personality. Elizabeth—according to Louise—had been on the verge of certified spinsterhood when Hugh showed up in Barbados and had married him within a month of their first meeting. It seemed that Elizabeth's parents had not thought to question Mattson's background. Had they been only too relieved that their daughter had found a British husband who could run the estate once they were gone?

In any case, over the twenty-some years of their marriage, Elizabeth seemed barely to have held her own, maybe only gradually claiming her independence prodded by her husband's infidelities and the knowledge of her own financial security. Witness the fact that she spent her trust fund on charitable works in obvious defiance of her husband. At the same time, she could not be oblivious to his mismanagement of her ancestral sugar plantation. Her discontent must have been augmented by her poor relationship with her daughter wherever the fault might lie.

Was her husband physically abusive? How, I wondered, would Elizabeth have dealt with that? From Louise's comments I had gathered that he was certainly emotionally abusive. Elizabeth had obviously turned to her religion for comfort and to Louise for friendship. Why had she agreed to go to Denmark? And had the vicar really pushed her into going sailing, an activity she abhorred?

I parked the car at the King's New Square. Birgit left me to walk to her newspaper near the town hall and I sauntered across to *Nyhavn*. I walked down the sidewalk past the long row of market umbrellas and the beer drinkers under them.

White fishing schooners were moored the length of the canal on both sides, even double parked, some appearing to be houseboats, others restaurants, with only a few looking like the real McCoy. A motorboat filled to capacity with windblown sightseers putt-putted down the middle of the waterway towards the landing steps at the beginning of the canal.

I was at the end of the sidewalk facing the widening canal leading out of the harbor and watched a large rusty oil tanker move leisurely towards the open sea. The salty mist in the air swept across my face and I closed my eyes listening to the far-off prolonged tooting of a ship's horns. A motorboat tugged along slowly nearby. I was just about to sit down on the stone fence at the embankment when I heard the tapping of wooden clogs behind me. Before I could turn around a body pressed against me and a huge hand closed around my left wrist. My arm was twisted behind my back, and cold steel dug into my midriff.

"Walk," said a familiar voice and Hugh Mattson pushed me across the sidewalk.

He held me close and goose-stepped behind me. I looked around wildly but I had left the crowded sidewalk cafés behind and the area was completely devoid of people.

I moved my right elbow in an effort to twist my body so I could punch his thigh and get out of the grip he had on my arm.

"Don't even think about it or you'll be dead in the water," he whistled in my ear and for a second I considered this option. I opened my mouth ready to let out one of my uncommonly piercing screams but we were now behind a large black van. Mattson pushed his knee violently into my back and flung me over the embankment and into the motorboat which I now realized had been following me all along.

Two arms caught me, a body weighted me down, and I fought with everything I had in me. I got up on all four, the body rolled off me and I rammed my head into a soft stomach. But before I could get up Mattson landed next to me with a thud. The other guy got up with a groan and tackled my legs enough to throw me off balance.

I screamed as loud as I'd ever screamed before in my life which only led to my being gagged with an oily cloth and punched in the stomach. I went temporarily limp. A few moments later I was covered from head to toe in a filthy blanket and trussed up with a thin nylon cord.

Jamie Prescott, lie low, get your wits about you. Think, think, think.

I willed myself to relax and breathe deeply through my nose. My throat felt dry. How could I have been so careless. I had seen him—and yet not seen him—after leaving Anton Christensen's apartment. Hugh Mattson's face had been moon shaped and clean shaven under his blue workman's cap, unrecognizable without the handlebar mustache and the wild sideburns. I remembered the sound of clogs and how he'd disappeared into a doorway when I turned around. He must have followed me to the hotel that first day. And today he must have trailed me from the hotel to *Vedbæk* and back to Copenhagen. No matter where he'd found me he must have planned to take me to the boat in *Nyhavn*.

The two arms which had caught me when I was thrown into the motorboat had belonged to Anton Christensen but

Hugh Mattson—or maybe I should now call him Hugo Madsen—was the one who barked orders in Danish. I could hear us splutter out of the canal, veer left, and speed up presumably into open water. Horns tooted in the far distance and soon all I heard and felt was the smooth chug-chugging of the boat. I worked my tongue around the oily cloth and managed to fight free of it. The clog bit into my side and I heard Hugh Mattson's muffled voice.

"Don't try anything," he said. As if I could.

I strained my muscles against the nylon cord and felt it give. I relaxed and tried it again but without result. It was simply too tight.

They're going to throw me overboard. The thought so rattled me that I started thrashing around in the blanket until I rolled over. It earned me another kick in the ribs.

The boat slowed down, purred along quietly, and turned in a wide circle. Then the engine was shut down and Mattson began to unbundle me. The pressure of the nylon cord around my body eased as the blanket was removed. My feet were strung together instead, and my arms were still tied behind my back. I could hardly come up with any kind of *tae kwon do* stance but I managed to hoist myself into a sitting position. My head was just above the side of the boat and when I looked around I saw only water. We were in the middle of the *Øresund* between Denmark and Sweden and the two shores were just distant lines.

I spat on the boards to rid myself of ill-tasting fluff from the blanket. I looked up and found Mattson and Anton peering into my face and I knew what was going to happen. They would dump me as I was, trussed up, and I'd have no earthly chance. It's hard to describe what went through my mind. All I knew was that I must talk myself out of it.

"Don't be foolish," I said to Mattson. "If you throw me overboard all tied up, it will never look accidental."

He didn't answer. He just tightened the cord around my wrists.

I decided to attack the weakest link.

"Don't let him drag you into this," I shouted to Anton Christensen. "You'll be a murderer. Not as harmless as pornography and child molestation. The police will soon find you."

"Hugo, let's cut her loose," Anton Christensen whined. "She's right. I'm scared."

"*Hun bluffer*," Hugh said in Danish and now, of course, I recognized that particular flat, colorless accent which he still had in English. Anton glared at me suspiciously.

"No," I said to him. "I'm not bluffing."

Anton let out a torrent of Danish, pointing first this way, then that. Mattson at first shook his head emphatically and argued back, then he listened and, finally, he acquiesced.

He was on his way towards me when we heard the whirring engine and then the loudspeaker. The boat had come upon us seemingly out of the blue. Coastguard, I thought, just as Mattson ducked, shoved the oily cloth back in my mouth, and covered me with the blanket.

The loudspeaker voice came across unintelligibly to me and Hugh Mattson answered in turn. This went on for a couple of interchanges while I tried to wiggle the oily cloth out of my mouth. It came out and I rolled over and kicked the blanket away ready to scream but knowing that only my appearance above the railing—and possibly my waving a white distress signal—would have any effect. I cried out in frustration and yanked at the nylon cord around my arms and legs to no effect whatsoever. And, at that moment, Hugh Mattson started the engine and we took off with a tremendous jerk which threw me against the side of the boat. The two men were busy maneuvering and I managed to raise my head above the railing before they took notice. The coastguard was heading away and we were pointed towards shore. But not for long. As soon as the coastguard was out of sight we slowed down and the engine was turned off.

"Time's up," Hugh Mattson said and pulled me up roughly. While he held me tightly from behind Anton

Christensen cut the line around my feet and then around my wrists. This was the moment I'd been waiting for.

I was free. I writhed out of Mattson's grip ducking under his arms to create space for my next move. I swung one elbow into his midriff. He groaned, lost his hold on me and veered sideways. In another split second I had struck out with my right foot at Anton Christensen and caught his kneecap. He collapsed against the railing without a sound, pivoted over the edge with arms flailing, and disappeared overboard.

I turned around but not quite fast enough. Mattson had grabbed something which I had no time to identify but which hurt when it bit into my ribcage. The tight space prevented him from swinging properly and the water-splashed deck caused him to slip. To my right I could now see Anton Christensen bobbing in the water, his arm stretched over his head in a mute cry for help, and just had time to wonder if Mattson would choose to help his cousin instead of pursuing me.

Mattson ignored Anton and quickly righted himself. He came at me with his bare hands. They looked like shovels and I had no time for complicated moves. Instead I did what I do well: I lunged for his left wrist, gripped it with both hands and twisted. I could hear it snap and let go.

I leaped towards the railing, hoisted myself upright, raised both arms, and jumped high and wide. Airborne, I had a triumphant feeling of success which lasted only until I hit the water. I stayed under and swam away from the boat for as long as I could which wasn't nearly long enough. As soon as I came up for air I heard the plopping sounds of bullets striking the surface of the water. Very close to my head.

I took in a huge gulp of air and held it while I let myself sink as far down as I dared. I swam underwater letting out my breath in tiny bubbles until I knew I would pass out if I didn't get back up. When I did, I took in another lungful of air, submerged myself again and continued swimming. I heard the distant noise of the motor and felt the vibrations in the water. I was rocked by the wake which soared around me in white turbulence and dared raise my head just long enough to locate the boat. It was now racing towards me.

But I knew that even if my head was above water it would be practically impossible for Mattson to keep his eye peeled on me in choppy water amidst white foam while steering the boat at the same time. But luck could still be on his side and I continued to gulp air and go under until the circles he made became wider and wider.

At the end Mattson circled back presumably to pick up Anton. Two boats came racing out of nowhere behind him but there was no way I could attract their attention. I had to watch them disappear. I turned on my back and floated to regain strength. It looked as if I was much closer to the Danish coast than to the Swedish. I wondered what the coastguard had told Mattson that had forced him to turn towards land. Whatever it was it had given me a small advantage.

The water was ice-cold and I knew I must move before my own temperature began to drop. I kicked off my sneakers which had filled with water, turned around and started my habitual fast crawl.

When after an eternity I turned on my back to float to prevent my legs from cramping up, the coast seemed no closer. I continued alternating between crawling and floating until the water turned warmer and I was close enough to the coast to see the houses on the bluff and the white strip of sand at the shore. Then I knew I would make it.

Ten minutes later I crept out of the water on my stomach without enough strength to stand up. I dragged across a narrow strip of sand to three steps leading to the road where I squatted on hands and knees before falling on my face.

I passed out.

CHAPTER 31

I looked up at several blurry faces. I tried to move my arm but I was hooked up to a bottle. I looked at my wrists and saw ugly red welts. Someone took my hand. Someone spoke. I didn't understand.

"Tusind tak," I muttered and closed my eyes while I recalled the water. And the cold. And Hugh Mattson. And Anton Christensen. I moaned and felt a needle in my arm. I conked out.

When I woke up the room was dark, only a night light glowed on the wall. I had a cord with a button lying across my chest and I kept my finger on the bell until a nurse appeared at the side of my bed.

"Water," I said and I didn't mean in the ocean. I drank several glasses while the nurse stood by with re-fills.

"Food," I said, and closed my eyes. When I opened them she had rolled a table across the bed and began to feed me spoonfuls of glue. Not oatmeal, I thought, and almost spat it out. But gradually it did make me feel better and I was able to chew on a piece of buttered toast and drink watered down tea.

"What happened," I asked.

"Hypothermia," she said. "Your temperature had gone way down. You were lucky someone found you and knew what to do."

"Who found me?"

"They didn't tell me."

I closed my eyes and tried to remember but couldn't.

When I woke up again, Mogens Hansen was sitting at my bedside. He was holding a huge bouquet of roses which he placed on the table when he saw me looking at him.

"Well, well, well," he said and I knew it was meant to cheer me up. But what I now wanted more than anything was an account of what had happened after I reached shore.

"How did you know I was here?" I said.

"You are very thorough," he said. "You had your money and passport and a slew of business cards, mine among them, in a plastic pouch inside your money-belt. Someone here called me immediately."

"Where are we?"

"At a medical facility near *Vedbæk*. The woman who brought you in her car had found you on the side of the road."

"The woman? Who was she?"

"I don't actually know. She didn't leave her name and she was gone before anyone could ask her."

"A nameless heroine," I mused. "I would have wanted to thank her."

Mogens Hansen nodded.

"Your cousin, Birgit Petersen, and a friend of yours, Bruno Halvorsen, are waiting outside to see you," he said. "I've pieced together some of the story from what they've told me and we've brought in Anton Christensen who was hiding out in the basement of his apartment building. Some school girls outside the house pointed us in the right direction. Seems he had some kind of perverted nest down there."

"Creep," I said with feeling.

"Claims he doesn't know a Hugh Mattson, claims he never left his apartment the day before yesterday, claims he's never set eyes on you. Since we couldn't prove anything we had to let him go."

"Creep," I said again and told Mogens Hansen the entire sequence of events from A to Z. He turned on a tape recorder when I began talking.

"We'll haul Christensen in again," he said, when I finished.

"And I take it Mattson has done another disappearing act?"

"We'll be working on it. In the meantime, my requests to morgues and hospitals for any Jane Doe's brought in the last six months have turned up nothing," he said. "We'll have to be patient."

He ought to know by now that patience is not my middle name, I thought.

Then, in short order, the nurse removed the IV, took my blood pressure and declared me ready to leave. Birgit handed me a paper bag with clean clothes from my closet at the hotel and a bouquet of flowers from her mother, Margrethe, and Bruno Halvorsen opened a box of chocolates which we shared with the nurses.

Birgit and Bruno Halvorsen left the room while I completed the paperwork which would discharge me from the facility.

"If the woman who brought me in should happen to call, please let me know," I said to the nurse. "I would like to thank her."

She put me in a wheelchair and pushed me to the exit door after I had paid my bill with some damp Danish kroner. Bruno Halvorsen and Mogens Hansen got into their separate cars and Birgit placed me in her old Peugeot and took me back to my hotel.

"I don't suppose you're up to going on the double date

I had lined up for to-night?" Birgit said when we were in my room. "No, of course, not," she answered her own question.
"You go, though," I said.
"You're sure you'll be all right? I hate to leave you but I also hate to give up my date with Jens. He's a new journalist on my paper, I've been waiting to go out with him." She laughed when she saw the unspoken question on my face. "And, yes, I'm through with Hans." She, apparently was able to read me just as clearly as Topsy could. What a curse to be born with such a baby-face, I thought.
"I assure you I'll be all right," I said. In fact I was rather wishing for her to go so I could get to my notes. The events of the past two days swirled through my head. I'm never able to collect my thoughts until they're written down. Today, however, I found myself staring at the empty page in dismay and soon had to give up.
But I knew where I would be going in the morning.

CHAPTER 32

The entrance to Anton Christensen's apartment building was even fouler than I remembered. Newspapers in the corner had fresh stains, and an open bag of garbage didn't help.

I climbed the stairs slowly without meeting anyone until the fifth floor where a woman opened her door and watched me through the crack. I felt her eyes following me until I disappeared around the last bend and heard her door click shut.

I put my hand across the spy hole on Anton Christensen's door before I rang the bell. The shuffling steps inside stopped and I imagined his eye encounter nothing but darkness. There was a long pause but I didn't hear his steps retreating. I kept my hand over the spy hole.

"Hugo?" he asked.

I didn't answer.

"Hugo?" he said again.

I made a sound between a cough and a snort and took my hand off the spy hole while ducking down so I couldn't be seen.

Slowly, the door opened a crack until it was caught by

the chain. Anton Christensen put his face close to the opening just as I sprang up from my crouched position, took a couple of steps back and put my shoulder to the door with as much force as I could muster. I've seen this done with excellent results in countless old movies without actually trying it myself.

The sound of splintered wood blending with loud cursing sounded promising but, in the end, the chain held in place and the door was slammed shut. I heard loud voices inside and a shadow passed across the spy hole. I put my finger on the door bell and kept it there. It was very shrill and someone inside shouted. I took my finger off the bell and put it back after about five seconds. Ten times in a row. I could hear the woman downstairs shouting something.

Then, without warning, the chain rattled and the door opened. Not waiting for an invitation I pushed and stepped inside practically into the arms of Anton Christensen. He had a cast on his leg where I'd broken his knee cap. His eyes were bloodshot but I couldn't take credit for that.

The door to the bedroom closed noiselessly, Anton smirked, but I decided I had bigger fish to fry than deal with his pedophile activities. He apparently had come to the same conclusion.

I walked into the living room and sat down on the stained couch. Anton sat down on a chair and actually smiled.

"I tried to help you," he said.

"You tried to *help* me?" I must have sounded furious because he drew back cautiously. "And just how did you do that?"

"I told him to cut the cord and set you free."

"Free?" I shouted. "Free to go where, to do what?"

"You kicked me overboard before I could help you." He stole a swift glance at me to see if I would buy it. Not! my expression must have said because he changed tactics. He pointed to the cast. "You broke my knee."

"He shot at me in the water," I said. By now we sounded like two kids having a fight.

I leaned back in my seat, crossed my legs and debated how best to get him to spill the beans. If he had any to spill, that is, and I wasn't even sure at this point.

"You were with Hugh Mattson when he pushed his wife overboard," I said.

I could tell from his stricken look that I'd hit home. He now looked scared.

"I have already told the police that I know nothing about that."

"And they believed you?" I laughed. "But, you see, I have information to the contrary. You're an accessory to murder."

"Accessory?"

"Equally responsible under the law."

"But I tried to help her!"

"Indeed? The same way you tried to help *me*?"

Having said too much, Anton Christensen now slumped in his chair.

"Are you going to tell them?" he said.

"No," I lied. "But it would be a good idea if you did. You must help the police to save your own skin." I could tell that he wouldn't have too much trouble with that concept.

"Did it happen in the same place?" I asked.

"No, closer to shore and not as far north."

"Tell me about it."

Anton heaved a big sigh and examined his grubby fingers after which he never once looked at me.

"Hugo, or Hugh, as you call him, disappeared from Denmark so many years ago that I thought he was dead. And when he suddenly showed up he was rich. He introduced me to his wife but invited me out to dinners and drinks without her. He said she'd gotten religion and couldn't enjoy the finer things in life. He always loved sailing and chartered a boat somewhere up the coast. Then he drove me up there with his wife. But she was a strange one. The minute we left the marina and before we were even in open water, she became hysterical and wanted Hugo to return.

"He got very angry and told her to sit in the cabin. When she started screaming he went in and gagged her with a towel. By then we had gone quite a few miles. She came out of the cabin and started to beat on him. And that's when it happened. Quite by accident, mind you. She fell overboard."

Anton Christensen shot me a furtive look and I shook my head.

"You'll have to do better than that," I said.

"I didn't see it. Not until she was in the water."

"And then?"

"Hugh turned the boat around and we returned to the marina. He put me ashore and went back out. I never saw him again until a week ago and that's the truth."

"And what did you imagine had happened to his wife?"

Anton averted his eyes.

"She drowned," he said.

"And you didn't think of reporting it?"

He shook his head and I got up. When I reached the tiny hallway, I stopped.

"You unspeakable worm," I said with feeling

I swirled around and Anton was quite unprepared. My knee found his groin and my fist landed in his face. I didn't mind the blood that spurted over my sleeve. When he was down I kicked his other kneecap. Very unsporting. He screamed.

"There you are," I said as I left. "What goes around, comes around."

On my way down the stairs the woman on the fifth floor cracked her door open and silently followed my descent.

Back at the hotel I called Mogens Hansen and half an hour later I was at the police station in his gray cell of an office. After I'd told him about my encounter with Anton Christensen he looked pleased.

"No good me telling you to take it easy," he said. "And with your cooperation we'll have a warrant for his arrest on more than one count. You'll also be glad to know that we've removed that young girl from his apartment."

"I'm sorry to disillusion you but I think she's back," I said. "And right now I'm more concerned about Hugh Mattson. He didn't even have to truss Elizabeth up. All he had to do was push her overboard. She couldn't swim. So why haven't we found her body? And without a body how can you convict Mattson? And where is he now?"

"A lot of good questions. To answer the last one first, we found the boat Mattson used. It could have been stolen from the harbor several days ago but the owner didn't realize it until that afternoon. His cell phone didn't work so he went to a café to call the police and report the theft. When he returned to the harbor the boat was back. He found some of the nylon cord they had used to tie you up. We managed to secure it."

"And Mattson? He must be long gone by now."

"Most likely he left by train. Anyone can board without a ticket and buy it en route. At the border down south they don't ask foreigners to submit passports. Anyone will sail right through. He could be anywhere in Europe by now. We'll get Interpol on the case."

"Could be a long while."

"Well, hopefully not. But, in fact, I was just about to call you when you reported in," he said.

It was quite late before we had sorted out all the details and I returned to the hotel.

Early the next morning I called Bob Makowski. He let out a long-drawn whistle when I told him about Hugh Mattson a.k.a. Hugo Madsen, and gave me all manner of flak about my near death experience. I told him the Danish police in the person of Mogens Hansen were on the ball.

"We need a resolution of the death certificate question, Bob."

"Well, my guy hasn't come through yet but I'll light

another fuse and get his sorry ass in gear." And on this note we hung up agreeing to wait another couple of days.

As it turned out, I didn't have to wait that long.

I called Louise Higginbotham who lifted the receiver as if she'd had her hand on it since I left Barbados. I could picture her in her dark-paneled agency, her head on the side, her eyes peering out the window at the perpetual Barbados sun—yet wrapped in her wool cardigan.

"I have news for you," she said. "You see, Elizabeth's death certificate was issued in St. Albans, Hertfordshire."

"How did you find out? Have you seen it?"

"No, but I have it on good authority."

"Did Bundy tell you?"

"No, for some reason he was not as efficient as I expected so, although I would have preferred not to annoy him, I went over his head, rather, to the Minister of the Interior. You see the minister is one of my dearest friends."

Of course, I thought.

"And the cause of death and the date," I said. "Did he tell you that?"

"Pneumonia, and the date was the 7th of August."

"Good job, Louise," I said with feeling.

"I'm sorry I wasted your time in Copenhagen," Louise said. "I've been rather overwrought lately and the uncertainty was difficult but now we have the answer and I feel relieved."

"I've got a few loose ends to tie up in Barbados," I said. "I'm leaving Copenhagen in a couple of days and will catch a British Airways flight to Barbados. But I'd rather we kept this to ourselves for the time being."

"Who would I tell," Louise said and I couldn't even begin to count the possibilities.

Next I caught Topsy in Bethesda on her way out of the agency. I gave her my account of happenings in Copenhagen but glossed over my Olympic swim in the straits between Denmark and Sweden.

"I know you're not telling me the whole truth," she said. "It's about time you came home. Frankly, I need you. Margo, of course, is gone. I'm doing the work of three travel agents and, in addition, Kristy quit on Friday. Not that I'd call what she did actual work."

"I'll make it up to you," I said. "We'll advertise as soon as I get back, we'll find two excellent replacements, and you'll take a vacation with Jack. I know you can't live without seeing him in your bed every morning."

"Sounds good," Topsy said. And then, "Archibald Brewster has moved back from San Francisco to the main law office in Washington." I could hear her listening for my reaction. And I'll admit that I did suck in my breath probably loud enough for her to hear.

"Thanks for being so concerned about my love life," I said. "But can you possibly restrain yourself and let me conduct this one on my own?"

"So, you'll see him again? Shall I tell him you'll call?"

"Topsy," I moaned.

"Just kidding."

I sat back in my Danish Modern sofa and thought about home and about Archibald Brewster. About his olive-skinned look. About his voice, his quick wit.

I started packing.

CHAPTER 33

I caught the earliest possible plane to London and on the following day the British Airways non-stop flight to Barbados.

It's a roller coaster, I thought, and looked down on the approaching white shoreline of Barbados. I wouldn't say that travel had been uneventful—the London airport alone had seen to that with its inevitable bus transfers and long walks to and fro—but at least we'd had no delays. I'd had plenty of time to update my notes and I now re-read them for the umpteenth time. I had a fairly good idea of my next actions. Being airborne usually clears any remaining fog in my brain. Today was no exception.

I had told Louise on the phone that I'd rather put the memory of my previous hotel and the burned cottage behind me and since I'd be arriving practically incognito I figured on taking a taxi to my new hotel. To this end I strode out of customs at *Grantley International Airport* confident in the remainder of my suntan, a Danish haircut, a minimal t-shirt, tight jeans, and high-heeled sandals. I felt seven feet tall.

"Va-Va-Voom!"

Mel Kramer, looking tanned and fit, teeth dazzling white, eyes deep violet, spread his arms in welcome and looked me up and down in that infuriating way of his.

I was back in Barbados.

"What are you doing here?" I probably sounded annoyed but, as usual, he didn't seem to notice.

"What do you mean, what am I doing here? Louise told me to pick you up."

I shook my head in disgust and then decided to relax. What had I been thinking anyway? That no one would know I had returned? That one word from Louise wouldn't have spread like wildfire? Even so, if I played my cards right I still had a slight advantage.

While Mel took up a position near the luggage belt I walked across to a public phone and called Louise. Again, it seemed that she was spending her life waiting for my calls. She picked up on the first ring. She invited me to dinner and said she'd fetch me at seven. I didn't mention Mel.

"*Ravissante!*" Jean-Pierre's voice was unmistakable. I twirled around and peered down at him from my added height. Then I looked around for Amaryllis, and maybe Bundy, or Beth, just to mention a few of the people I didn't want to see. Apart from that I'd have to stop my heart from skipping beats at the sight of a curly beard.

"*Mon Dieu,* I thought I'd never see you again," he said. "Why have you come back?"

That's for me to know and for you to discover, I thought, and answered his question with one of my own.

"What are *you* doing at the airport?"

"Just picking up some spare-parts from England."

"And how is Amaryllis?" I said and enjoyed his discomfited look and the way he turned around anxiously.

But before he could answer Mel walked up with my suitcase and took my arm.

"Say goodbye," he said to Jean-Pierre and grinned.

"Bastard," he said to me when we were out of earshot on our way to the parking lot. "Noelle and I have split up."

"You've split up? What, because of him?" And I pointed towards the arrival hall.

"Not entirely." Mel put the car in gear and we lumbered out of the airport towards Route 1 going North. I'd forgotten about the Barbados speed limits. But this time I couldn't afford to be lulled into slow motion either physically or mentally. I needed to keep my wits about me.

"She moved out," he said. "I'm selling the art gallery. I just need to sign one more document and it's a done deal."

"I'm stunned," I said. "I had no idea." I realized how little I'd understood their relationship. I tried in a few seconds to reconstruct it in my mind. The comradeship, the physical attraction. Then, the obvious boredom, the differences in age and culture. But still. "I'm sorry," I said.

"Don't be sorry. I'm ready to move on," Mel said, and I froze at the sudden notion that he might be thinking of moving on with me.

"Who bought the gallery?"

"A group of locals."

"Will you be staying on in Barbados?"

"Don't know. I haven't quite decided what to do. I'll be in New York in a couple of weeks to look into some possibilities there."

I hadn't, of course, packed my red and white striped itsy bitsy bikini going to Copenhagen, so I instructed Mel to stop on Main Street in Bridgetown and wait while I—once more—replenished my beach wardrobe, this time in my own size.

Mel accompanied me to my new hotel—less pretentious than the previous one—and sat with me on the porch with a rum punch until I nodded off in my chair. He left reluctantly to let me cope with my jet lag.

I woke up at six in the evening feeling, if not fresh as a daisy, then sufficiently restored to go for a swim. My room faced the beach and it was a short three steps down from the porch to the sand. The surface was calm, the water lukewarm, the sun was sinking towards the horizon, and I lay there on my back being rocked gently by the undertow, recalling previous events.

Louise picked me up at seven and took me to her house where we dined alone on Cajun shrimp, rice, a green salad and, surprisingly, bread pudding with treacle. It would help me sleep through the night—or not—I thought and swallowed the last heavy spoonful.

Then we sat down in her living room and I told her what had happened. She never once interrupted me. When I came to the end of my story she just sat there looking very pale.

"Keep all this strictly to yourself for a couple of more days," I said at last. And I knew that this time she would.

"What shall we do about Amaryllis?" she asked.

"You must let me handle it," I said."I will pay her a visit."

I got up and Louise took me back to my hotel.

Tomorrow would be one busy day.

CHAPTER 34

"What do you hear from Noelle?" I asked when Mel picked me up the next morning.

"She's in the Dominican Republic looking for an art gallery."

"You're definitely putting it behind you?"

"Sure." Mel sounded surprisingly upbeat. "But enough about me. Tell me about your adventures in Copenhagen. Louise has suddenly clammed up and she usually has loose lips. But she did tell me about the missing boarding pass stub."

I shouldn't have been surprised. That's why, even now, I hadn't told Louise everything. Charming as she was she simply couldn't be trusted.

"And who else did she tell?" I said.

"No one, I imagine, although I don't see what all the secrecy is about? Some kind of private investigator thing no doubt." Mel poked his elbow into my ribs. "Do you mind if we pass by the gallery on our way to the plantation? I want a word with the new owners. We still need to sign one more document of transfer."

"I don't mind." In fact, at the prospect of confronting Amaryllis I didn't mind stalling.

Bridgetown had that quiet atmosphere of 'nothing bad ever happens here.' Tourists milled about looking hot and busy. Bajans walked and talked leisurely, looking cool and breezy. White-helmeted police officers pivoted on tippy-toe and held up the lethargic traffic for pedestrians. Fruit vendors sat under market umbrellas next to papayas, mangos, and bananas. We passed Louise Higginbotham's travel agency where the window display had not improved since the first time I saw it. Mel parked outside the *Sunshine Art Gallery* and I hopped out with him. The sign now said *Owner: A. Justin*.

"What the hell is that?" Mel stared through the plate glass window.

"Oh, my God!" I shouted at the same time and pushed him aside.

Prominently displayed, on an easel, stood my Haitian Préfète Duffaut painting.

I pulled Mel to the side so we couldn't be seen from the gallery.

"That's my painting!"

"How did it get here?"

"Someone wanted me out of the way and burning down my cottage was supposed to make me leave. Maybe the painting was just a bonus. A lucrative one."

I dragged Mel back to the car and he pulled away from the curb and around the corner where he stopped.

"Let's think," he said.

"What's to think about? It's very clear. It's mine and I want it back. Got your gun?"

Mel didn't even blink and I had no time to explain how I knew he had one.

"Sure, right here." He snapped open the glove compartment. "It's not loaded, of course."

"No one will know. Ready?"

"You're on!"

"Let's go!"

Mel made a U-turn and in two minutes had us back in front of the gallery.

There were no customers, just a tall man and a very large woman at a desk against the back wall. The woman, who had her back to us, was in a bright red dress with a matching flower in her hair. The man looked expensive in a silk suit and tie. When he turned around his eyes popped, and so did mine.

"Hugh Mattson's handyman," I whispered to Mel.

"What handyman? He's the son of the Minister of Culture. His name is Antoine."

"I saw him load Mattson's boat."

"No way." Mel sounded so definitive that my conviction wavered. I must be mistaken. It's true he looked different in a suit but I felt pretty sure he'd recognized me, too.

The woman came forward and she was no longer in a maid's uniform and apron with a bandanna over her hair.

"Jeanette, my substitute maid," I said to Mel.

"What do you mean, maid? Her name's Poupette, she's his wife, she's from Martinique, and he calls her *Petite*."

"No, no, she's from Haiti and 'petite' she ain't."

"She's from Martinique," Mel repeated. "And she's Noelle's cousin."

Confused, I looked around the gallery. The walls were colorful with exotic pictures hanging from floor to ceiling. And there—in the middle—were two more Haitian paintings—both mine.

Mel whipped out his gun and waved it at Antoine who sidled backwards and cowered behind Petite. She glared at me with hostile eyes. No more servility here. I'd have to straighten this out later, I thought, although I now had little doubt where to point the finger.

"What's the problem?" Antoine shouted.

"Thievery and arson and a helluva lot more," Mel shot back. "You're in big trouble, my friend, no matter who your father is. And you can kiss the gallery goodbye. Let's go. Into the back office. And put your cell phones right here on the desk."

Petite moved reluctantly and I could tell her little gray cells were working out an escape route. But Antoine pushed her towards the stockroom glancing nervously at the gun which Mel waved about nonchalantly.

"There we go," Mel said, and shoved the gun in Antoine's back. I was close behind them and when the two were inside, I deftly removed the key, slammed the door shut, and locked it from the outside.

Mel and I looked at each other and grinned. And grinned some more.

"You're a hell of a woman," he said. "A cut above."

"Fun, wasn't it?" I gave him the key. "Here, you be the jail-keeper."

Mel quickly removed my painting from the window and replaced it with one from the wall. I took down my other two paintings and walked with them to the front door.

"I can't believe they kept the evidence in clear view. They were sure I'd left the island for good," I said.

"The morons. They should have realized that *I* would recognize the paintings."

Mel turned the sign in the window to *Closed* and we exited quickly. Mel locked the door from the outside and gave me a high-five.

"I'll let them out later. That'll give them time to think up some improbable story. Right now, it's off to the plantation we go. But first, let's stop by my house."

Exactly five minutes later we were in his living room stripping the three painting from their binder frames. Mel rolled up the canvases, wrapped them in one of Noelle's sexy pillow-cases, put them in the trunk of his car, and we were back going North on Route 1 at fifty miles an hour.

A cell phone rang faintly above the clamor of traffic.

"It's not mine," Mel said, and I rooted around in my backpack. By the time I found it, it had stopped ringing. I looked at the screen but couldn't locate the promised incoming message.

"Damn phones," Mel said. "Never work."

The Bajan landscape flew by and the cows on the sides of the highway looked startled and stopped chewing.

CHAPTER 35

We turned off the main road to go inland, down the winding lanes lined with sugarcane and banana plants, with dust rising behind the car, and Copenhagen felt far away and quite unreal. There was the sugar mill with its huge crane swinging slowly, then dropping to scoop up the cane on the ground. No one was around, maybe they were still in the fields we had passed. We drove by the manager's house but, as usual, Jean-Pierre was not there.

At the end of the tree-lined avenue the mansion stood behind its stone wall, the coral block facade glinting in the sunlight. The windows arched high, the red tiled roof showed off the many chimneys. The courtyard stretched towards the front door. I was back at the Granger-Farley sugar plantation.

No cars were parked in front of the entrance, and the iron gate which had been locked and chained on my last visit now stood open. After leaving the car and walking into the courtyard, Mel and I stood a moment side by side staring up at the dark, closed windows where no curtains fluttered invitingly. The place looked deserted and the front door was locked. I looked for a bell but Mel lifted the heavy knocker and pounded vigorously.

We waited and Mel knocked again.

The silence outside was profound and there were no sounds from the inside so, when the door was suddenly flung open, I took a step back, startled.

"Why, it's you, you bloody woman," Amaryllis shouted and took a menacing step towards me. I must say I was quite tired of being the bloody woman but remembering her unpredictable behavior and our previous fight in the cemetery, I held my tongue.

"Now, that's no way to talk," Mel said in a scolding voice which might have worked on a three-year old but certainly had no effect on Amaryllis.

"What do *you* want?" she hissed at him. "I suppose you want Noelle but she isn't here and I don't care if I ever see her again. Good riddance to bad rubbish, that's what *I* say."

By now Mel and I had insinuated ourselves inside the foyer and Amaryllis had apparently decided she didn't mind our company after all.

"I thought you and Noelle were friends," Mel said and looked genuinely surprised. "What's she ever done to you except being helpful?"

"And are *you* looking for Noelle, too?" Amaryllis eyed me with contempt. "I thought you'd left the island but you probably couldn't keep away from Jean-Pierre."

I was just about to tell her how tiresome she was when high heels clicked and I turned around to find Noelle coming in the front door. She looked alarmed for a fraction of a second as her eyes swept across our many faces. She held up her hand as if to warn off somebody. The somebody turned out to be Chief Inspector Bundy. Oh, good, I thought, now all we need is Beth and the party is complete.

"*Mon amour*," Noelle said to Mel in a cool voice.

"Isn't that something of a misnomer?" Mel looked sour. "What are you doing here, you said you were going to the Dominican Republic."

"A girl can change her mind, can't she? I had some unfinished business here."

"No doubt with your new boyfriend."

Noelle turned her attention to me.

"Hello, *mà chérie*, I heard a rumor that you'd returned to the island. Was Copenhagen everything you hoped for?"

How the heck did everyone know my every step, my every action? I ignored Noelle and turned to Amaryllis.

"What do you hear from your father?" I said. "I understand he has left for England again?"

"None of your bloody, bloody business," Amaryllis said and her face took on the hue of her spiked hair. "But here comes the man you're making yourself a fool over. Trust me, he's not in the market for a tight-assed woman fifteen years older."

I decided to ignore the tight-ass remark. But fifteen? What a nerve.

Jean-Pierre stood in the doorway staring at us and, to his credit, looked quite embarrassed. He also looked as if he was about to turn and flee. But Amaryllis was at his side in a few well-placed steps, put her arm through his and dragged him inside.

"Where have you been," she said in a low voice but not so low that we couldn't hear her. "You said you'd be here last night."

Jean-Pierre faked a cough attack, disengaged his arm and spluttered noisily into a Kleenex. He went through to the library door and then, presumably, to the bathroom at the end of the hall. Amaryllis followed him swiftly.

And that was the moment Louise Higginbotham chose to make her entrance. She turned to someone behind her and ushered in a blond woman carrying a small suitcase.

"Look what I found next to a collapsed taxi up on the road," she said. "She was on her way to the plantation so I offered her a ride. This is Nancy."

"Hello," the woman said. "Nancy François, actually. I'm looking for Jean-Pierre."

"Oh, my dear," Louise said. "I didn't realize you were a relative of his. A sister, perhaps?"

She was pale, short, in her late twenties, with sharp blue eyes, eyes rather like a hawk. Not the looks one would have expected but, of course, siblings had genes from two parents and could be unbelievably dissimilar.

"Sister? I don't think so," she said and speared us with her hawk's eyes. "I'm his wife."

"Oh, no," Mel exclaimed, and I couldn't tell if he was laughing or crying. "A little wifey. Let me go get Jean-Pierre. He'll be *so* surprised and *I* want to be the one to tell him."

Lead had invaded my legs and Noelle and Louise looked as if they, too, were glued to the floor. Only the debonair Bundy looked oblivious.

I could hear Mel's animated voice and Jean-Pierre answering him. Then the brisk steps stopped abruptly. They stood in the doorway from the library with Amaryllis between them.

"*Mon Dieu*," came the strangled outcry and Jean-Pierre shrank back.

"Surprise," said the wifey.

"*Nancy!*"

"Jean-Pierre," said Louise and beamed at them. "She was stranded on the road on her way here. If I'd known she was your wife we could have gone straight to your house. You must have missed her so much. I hope she has come to stay. And I want you to bring her over for tea very soon."

I'm not sure Jean-Pierre heard her because the next I saw of him was his back, the small suitcase in his hand, Nancy trailing behind him, and Amaryllis shouting obscenities at them both.

"Sure made my day." Mel's eyes shone with *schadenfreude*. Amaryllis slumped down on a chair looking like a child who'd just lost her lollipop. Noelle tossed her head as if to say 'there are more fish in the sea.' Louise looked bewildered, and I whistled under my breath and thought 'he jumped up like a lion and fell down like a lamb.'

"I'll get it," Noelle said when the phone rang in the library. Her heels clicked hard until she slammed the door shut and we couldn't hear her voice. She returned after several long minutes and walked straight over to Amaryllis.

"Your father's on the phone from England," she said. "He wants to talk to you."

England, my foot, I thought.

When they returned to the foyer where Louise and Mel and I were still standing I scrutinized their faces for signs that Hugh had told them about my demise in the dark waters of the *Øresund* but Noelle and Amaryllis looked quite unperturbed.

In spite of recent events I suddenly felt in complete control. I heard a car door slam and turned to my ill-assorted company.

"Let's go sit down in the library," I said and held the door open. "I have something to tell you."

Louise led the way, her Roman nose held high, eyes looking straight ahead. Noelle hesitated briefly, but followed with Bundy at her heels. Mel, looking rather solicitous, brought in an unusually subdued Amaryllis and I left the door ajar. They all sat down and looked at me expectantly. I remained standing with my back to the door.

The voice came from the foyer and Amaryllis started to get up. Louise sniffed and her nostrils vibrated. Mel and Noelle rose simultaneously. Our heads turned.

And there she stood—not lost but calm—dressed in a new summer dress, a wool cardigan, and sturdy shoes.

Elizabeth Granger-Farley Mattson had returned from the dead.

CHAPTER 36

Pandemonium broke loose in the library. Amaryllis cried hysterically. Louise rushed about like a headless chicken. Mel shouted inanities, and Noelle and Chief Inspector Bundy stayed uncharacteristically in the background while I thought of the events of my last couple of days in Copenhagen.

I had rushed along to the police station after my confrontation with Anton Christensen.

"Hugo Madsen left Denmark twenty-three years ago," Mogens Hansen said when I arrived. "He had serious charges against him. Wounded a security guard during an armed robbery. Escaped while being transfered from the courthouse to prison after which he disappeared. He apparently stayed in England a couple of years, obtained a forged British passport, became an Englishman named Hugh Mattson, and shipped to Barbados where he stayed and, well, you know the rest."

Mogens Hansen had looked at me strangely.

"You have done well," he said. "We would never have gotten this far if not for you."

"Probably not," I said. False modesty is not my gig.

And then he told me. A report had just come in from a hospital north of Copenhagen about a woman suffering from amnesia. She had been found wandering the streets of Elsinore, without any information on her person to reveal her identity. She refused to speak.

We had arrived at the hospital within half an hour.

The woman was in a bed, her hands fidgeting on top of the blanket. Her eyes were closed, her hair hung down the sides of her face, her lips moved as if in prayer. Then she opened her eyes and looked around the room in apparent confusion.

"Hello," I had said. "My name is Jamie and I have just arrived from Barbados. Are you Elizabeth?"

She had stretched out her hand to me.

"Have you come to take me home?" she said. "I want to go home."

"She's not Danish! She speaks English!" the nurse had exclaimed. "She has not spoken before."

It was hard for me now, even just a week later, to recall my stupefaction, the sense of unreality which suddenly enveloped me. My immense relief and, at the same time, a certain outrage. Mogens Hansen dug up the truth through some hard questioning of the nursing staff. The paperwork reporting Elizabeth's appearance to the authorities had somehow been lost in a drawer. It appeared that Elizabeth had been at the hospital for several weeks.

In the end Elizabeth had stayed another few days at the hospital. She regained her bodily strength amazingly quickly. She was diagnosed with trauma-induced amnesia so severe that even her personal identity had been forgotten. It was thought that a history of emotional and physical trauma—or hippocampal-temporal lobe injury—had predisposed her to suffer a complete memory loss and that she would never completely remember what had happened. She could not recall where she had been those several months and how she came to wear clothes with Danish tags. And sturdy Danish walking shoes.

Thanks to Mogens Hansen's intervention the consular section of the High Commission of Barbados in London issued Elizabeth a new passport. We traveled to London together and over-nighted in style at Claridge's. I left for Barbados early the next morning while Elizabeth stayed one more day to allow me to prepare the grounds for her arrival. Her friend, the Minister of the Interior—who had been specifically instructed not to tell Louise—had sent a car to whisk Elizabeth from the airport directly to the plantation.

Now, there was dead silence in the room. Amaryllis, white under her tan, sat frozen before she got up and walked slowly to her mother. I noticed in wonderment that she didn't embrace her but just stood in front of her, subdued. Maybe it was the old British stiff upper lip but, more likely, it was due to a bad conscience. After a tense moment, Elizabeth put her arms around her daughter and held her. And then everyone talked in a babble of voices.

Elizabeth sat down next to Louise who still looked very pale indeed. Elizabeth's return was the one thing I hadn't told my loose-lipped friend.

"Hugh threw me overboard," Elizabeth stated simply and she was no longer the meek little woman. Her back was straight, her shoulders squared and, right there, she grew in front of our eyes.

"You should know that our marriage was finished. He was squandering my inheritance. I had told Hugh I wanted a divorce, I could no longer tolerate his immoral and criminal behavior. I discovered drugs and prostitution. I told him I would inform the police if he didn't give me the divorce."

Elizabeth had already told me why she agreed to accompany Hugh to England and Denmark and now she told the others.

"I was nevertheless in grave doubt. Divorce is against everything I believe in. And Hugh swore he would reform.

He became very attentive. I wanted to trust him. And when we were in Copenhagen the Anglican vicar was so persuasive. I fought to overcome my phobia about sailing. I desperately wished to do what God wanted."

Louise took her hand and squeezed it.

"Hugh threw me from that odious boat, turned it around and fled. I prayed to my Savior to help me and he answered my prayers. He sent me a wooden plank to which I clung. I may not be able to swim, but I know how to cling. I still can't remember what happened to me after that. Then, after a long time, there was Jamie Prescott looking at me and speaking in English, and suddenly my mind snapped back in place and I remembered who I was."

I smiled to myself and Mel raised an eyebrow at me. I had been picturing the newly confident Elizabeth Mattson, the owner of a soon-to-be prosperous diversified crop plantation traveling with Louise on exciting excursions around the world—safaris in Africa, gambling in Las Vegas, gondolas in Venice. Now I got up.

"It's time we left," I said. "I'm sure Elizabeth needs her rest."

"I'll stay," Louise said. "I'm still wobbly from the shock. I thought you were dead, Elizabeth. Hugh said you died in England and he brought back your death certificate issued in St. Albans, Hertfordshire."

"Yes, I heard," said Elizabeth dryly. "He always was a cheat."

Mel and I stood outside with Noelle and Bundy looking at the two available cars and Mel, after some hesitation, steered Bundy to his.

"You take Jamie," he said to Noelle who looked conflicted but gave in with just one ambivalent stare at Bundy.

"I'll see you later," I said to Mel.

"Let's go," Noelle said.

CHAPTER 37

I walked around to the passenger side of Noelle's car and waited for her. She opened her door and swore softly under her breath.

"*Merde*, I dropped the keys," she said and circled around searching. In the several moments it took her, Mel's car had vanished down the driveway.

"Ah, here they are. Ready to go," she said and started the car. Our headlights swung in a wide arc across the sugarcane fields and lit up the narrow road where the hedges cast weird shadows. I knew I wouldn't return here in a hurry, if ever, and I can't say I was sorry.

"I met your cousin, Petite, and her husband, Antoine, this morning," I said. "They had some interesting paintings on display."

Noelle braked and tooted the horn at a flock of sheep crossing the road.

"*Mon Dieu*," she shouted and righted the car.

I stared out the window and we drove on in silence. Just when the quiet had become thoroughly oppressive Noelle blurted out:

"You certainly had a busy time in Copenhagen. And imagine Elizabeth showing up alive. I can't believe Hugh dumped her overboard deliberately. Her memory must be playing tricks on her. It must have been an accident."

"It was no accident," I said. "And I'll say the same for the three drownings and the disappearance of Andy Harris."

"*Eh, bién,* you are probably right. But I would leave it up to Bundy to figure out. That's his job. For myself, I will be glad to leave this island. I am ready to move on." Her words were strangely reminiscent of Mel's.

"I think you may want to know a little more about Hugh," I said. "Right now he's on the run somewhere in Europe pursued by Interpol and, once caught, will be extradited to Denmark on charges of attempted murder."

She turned to look at me.

"The only proof they have is the statement of a demented woman," she said. "I wouldn't worry too much if I were you."

"Two attempted murders, actually, and there's no way they will discount *my* story," I said.

The car swerved as Noelle almost lost her grip on the wheel.

"What *are* you talking about, *chérie?*"

"Hugh Mattson has a one-track mind. He rented a boat to take Elizabeth sailing, he threw her overboard quite close to shore knowing she couldn't swim. He kidnapped me in a stolen boat, sailed about the same distance north and threw me in near the same shore. If it hadn't been for the interference of the coastguard he would have dumped me in the middle of the strait. From there I might not have made it."

"I don't believe a word of that."

"I don't see why not. Hugh Mattson is not a very intelligent man. But he's a very greedy man and since he couldn't lay his hands on his wife's money he'd turned to something more obvious. His wife threatened to denounce him for drug smuggling. His lucrative yachting excursions were in danger. His accomplices put pressure on him to silence her and someone suggested a neat scheme to him."

"What scheme are you talking about?"

"A scheme of deception, of forgery, of murder."

"Now who would that someone be?"

"Someone devious, someone persuasive. Someone who had a high stake in the operation."

"And do you know who that someone is?"

"I've got a good idea. And when Hugh is caught he'll no doubt confirm it."

Again, silence descended on us and I jumped when Noelle's cell phone pealed like Big Ben. She said 'hello' a couple of times, shook her head and hung up. The road was empty of traffic and we speeded up past large houses set back up the hills. That rapid tropical darkness quickly encircled us and the beam lit up the road in a single short burst. We slowed down.

And that was when Noelle swung the car sharply to the right and we went down a steep incline towards the beach. I was jolted hard against the door. She stopped the car and turned to me.

Something glinted in her hand and I looked into the business end of a revolver.

"Now drop your gun on the floor," she said.

"My gun?" I tried.

"Yes, I'm not stupid. Drop it."

I got Mel Kramer's gun out of my pocket and dropped it on the floor. Mel had been in turn incredulous and outraged and, finally, furious that Noelle had duped him. He had loaded his gun and given it to me during our sojourn to his house but it wasn't going to help me now.

"I want it under the seat," Noelle said, and I kicked it under.

"Don't move," she said and brought her left hand across to release my seatbelt. "Now, turn sideways and put your hands on top of your head."

She opened her door, sidled out, kept the gun pointed at my head and motioned me to slide across to the driver's seat and out on her side of the car.

The beach was now pitch black, the moon had not come out, and the waves whooshed noisily on their outward journey. Noelle had chosen a completely deserted strip of beach with clumps of banana plants. The thick leaves swayed in the evening breeze and cast billowing shadows across the sand.

The man came out of those shadows like an alley cat.

"Here," Hugh Mattson said and took the gun from Noelle. "I'll handle it from here on."

"You don't want to do this," I shouted to Noelle.

"Want to bet? You've been a monumental pain in the ass since you got here. I've had enough of you."

"Keep your hands on top of your head. We're walking." Mattson shoved me forward. His left arm was in a cast where I had broken his wrist before diving overboard into the Øresund.

When I took only a small step forward he pushed me viciously.

"Five steps ahead of me," he said. "I can assure you I'll shoot. I have an important date to keep."

I walked five steps ahead of them as ordered but turned my head so Noelle could hear me.

"You won't get away with this," I said. "You don't imagine I have left myself entirely at your mercy? I had a pleasant chat with the Minister of the Interior and your pal Bundy this afternoon. Bundy caved immediately and pointed the finger at you for my accident on the east coast. He also revealed the identity of the three drowned guys—from New Zealand—who, like Andy, got too ambitious and tried to muzzle in on your drug distribution network."

"Shut your mouth." Hugh ordered.

"You had this set up in Martinique," I continued to Noelle. "When things got hot there you moved your operation to Barbados and recruited Bundy. He agreed to bring you to the plantation today in return for leniency."

"And I suppose you were going to bring *me* in driving my own car?" The wind carried Noelle's derisive voice up in the air and I had to admit to myself that my scheme had not worked out entirely as planned. The idea had been for Bundy to drive Noelle to the plantation and return to town alone, while Mel and I would drive Noelle straight to the police station. Instead, Noelle had insisted on driving her own car, Bundy hadn't managed to alert me, Mel had confused the plan further by leaving me alone with Noelle and, as the saying goes, the rest was history.

"I'll handle her," Hugh Mattson said to Noelle.

"No, you won't. You'll mess it up, as usual." Her voice was furious. "Why did you come back? I told you to stay away."

"And you thought I'd let you walk off with all the money?" Hugh waved the gun in her direction. "No one knows I'm here."

"Give me back the gun," she screamed and while they yelled at each other I slowly moved sideways and was about to zig-zag away knowing that I could out-run both of them—even taking a chance on dodging bullets in the dark—when Hugh turned back to me.

He cocked the gun and trained it on me.

"Get down to the boat. Now," he yelled to Noelle. "And, remember, my men will see to it that you don't take off without me"

Defeated, Noelle kicked off her high heels and I saw her silhouette flailing away at the water's edge.

Hugh Mattson poked the gun in my back and I stumbled into a hole in the sand. I fell sideways twisting my ankle and let out an entirely genuine moan.

He waved the gun in my face.

"Get up," he hissed. "Let's go. We're sailing out of here."

I now saw the shadow of the pier and the dark mass of Beth's diveshop. I stumbled forward bearing down on my ankle which already felt painfully swollen.

I tripped again and pitched forward onto my knees. Hugh stepped up close and bent down. That was all I needed. I wrapped both arms around his legs and tripped him. He rolled sideways, I ignored my twisted foot, rose to full height and hurtled myself on top of him.

That's when the gun went off. The sound was deafening in the still evening air. Mattson twisted under me and I was covered in blood. My body stiffened and I rolled away from him but the scream that filled the air wasn't mine.

Going down, Hugh Mattson had shot himself in the leg. Blood gushed from the wound and I knew he'd need a tourniquet. But first I'd have to deal with Noelle.

She came running back out of the dark as suddenly as she had disappeared a few moments ago.

"Hugh," she screamed. "You idiot. Why didn't you wait until you got her on the boat."

She stopped when she saw me with Hugh's gun. She took one look at him on the ground, another at me, turned and ran.

"Beth," she screamed. "Wait for me."

But Beth wasn't about to wait. I saw her scramble out of her hut, onto the pier, and a moment later an engine spluttered and the speedboat roared out to sea towards Hugh's yacht. Beth would be going it alone. Until she climbed onboard and met up with the coastguard waiting there courtesy of the Minister of the Interior.

Noelle wouldn't get far either.

I tore off my t-shirt, wrapped it around Mattson's leg just above the knee and twisted it into a hard knot. The blood stopped gushing. His face was pale under a dark five o'clock shadow. I searched his pockets and found his cell phone. His worked where mine wouldn't. Mel answered.

He was waiting for me a mile away, as it turned out. I described my location and waited for him and Bundy to backtrack. We carried Mattson up the incline to the road—

heavy going for me in deep sand with a swollen ankle—and got him into the back seat of the car next to Bundy.

Mel looked me over.

"Sexy bra," he said, and I got into the passenger seat.

"Thanks," I said and caught the sweatshirt he tossed me. I pulled it over my head.

Twenty minutes later we delivered Hugh Mattson to the emergency room where he was admitted under the supervision of Bundy's successor—the new Chief Inspector.

Mel drove me back to the hotel but didn't get out of the car. He turned to me and took my hand.

"Are you okay?"

"I'm good," I said. "I'm real good. But what about you?"

"I'm not that good," he stated flatly. He released my hand. "I guess you'll be leaving tomorrow?"

"Absolutely." I got out of the car and started walking. "This has been the vacation from hell."

EPILOGUE

The headline in the *Barbados Advocate* appeared the way I feared. This time the police had immediately identified Andy.

While I was in the car with Noelle on our last ride together, Mogens Hansen had tried unsuccessfully to leave a message on my cell phone to the effect that Hugh Mattson had been traced to London booking a flight to Barbados. It could have saved me a lot of grief.

Hugh is now keeping Noelle and Beth company in prison somewhere on the island while Bundy has retired from the police force.

In Copenhagen, Anton Christensen has been charged with corruption of minors.

Jean-Pierre and his wife, Nancy, help Elizabeth run her plantation. She tells me Nancy is keeping him on a tight rope. That makes me laugh. I know it won't take Jean-Pierre long to worm his way out of it.

Hugh's "housekeeper," Mirabelle, left the plantation without anyone noticing and is back behind the bar at the cricket club.

Louise Higginbotham is planning an elaborate travel schedule around the world with Elizabeth.

Amaryllis is attending cooking classes in Switzerland and has taken up skiing. She never writes her mother.

Mel sold the *Sunshine Art Gallery* to an expatriate American couple, returned to New York and moved in with his old girlfriend, a graphic artist from Norway.

I've located one of my mother's first cousins living, if you please, at the ancestral manor house south of Stockholm. She has invited us to visit some time in the future.

Birgit plays the field in Copenhagen and Hans is still in India.

At the airport Bob Makowski took one look at my swollen ankle and the British gent's walking stick given me by Louise, shook his head and wisely refrained from comment.

Topsy nixed the scuba-diving tours in Barbados. She arranges no more blind dates. She says I'm going steady with Archibald Brewster but I wouldn't go that far.

I like to keep my options open.

CPSIA information can be obtained at www.ICGtesting.com
Printed in the USA
LVOW12s2140121114

413436LV00001B/55/P